BANGALORS

CARL E. BOYETT

authorHOUSE'

AuthorHouse™
1663 Liberty Drive
Bloomington, IN 47403
www.authorhouse.com
Phone: 833-262-8899

Published by AuthorHouse 08/14/2023

ISBN: 979-8-8230-1325-3 (sc)
ISBN: 979-8-8230-1324-6 (e)

Library of Congress Control Number: 2023915193

Print information available on the last page.

Any people depicted in stock imagery provided by Getty Images are models, and such images are being used for illustrative purposes only. Certain stock imagery © Getty Images.

This book is printed on acid-free paper.

------------------ C H A P T E R   1 ------------------

creation of a world

In the late twenty-first century, a rogue nation on planet Earth launched nuclear warheads at several nations. Those nations retaliated in kind by launching their own warheads. These actions led to a global war that wiped out nearly half the planet's population. After this conflict, what remained of the different governing bodies joined together to rebuild Earth. They used technology and science, conferred with what experts remained, and worked to clean the atmosphere and water of pollutants, thus eradicating the land of nuclear waste. The population of the planet migrated to cleaner more habitable areas, leading to catastrophic food shortages. The government and scientists, devoid of a plan, turned to the stars for answers. With the development of spaceships that could travel at light speed, they encouraged people to venture outside of the solar system to look for inhabitable planets and colonize new worlds. So the people of Earth began to move off into the universe, settling on unpopulated planets and merging into the culture of planets that already had populations.

"So, Mr. Robertson, does that answer your question about how our planet became populated?

"Yes, ma'am," replied the skinny Theodore Robertson.

"Sked," whispered Tyler Pickings to Caalin. Sked is the name kids call the students that ask questions to get the attention of the teachers to make points with them, sort of a teacher's pet. Caalin chuckled, and Ms. Wandon quickly asked, "Mr. Matthews do you have something you would like to share with the class?" "No, ma'am, just clearing my throat," he answered.

A young boy entered the classroom with a note for Ms. Wandon. She took the note, read it, and looked up at Caalin with a little smile. "It seems Mr. Matthews, the Dean of Students, would like to see you in his office."

Caalin rose from his desk and followed the boy out the door and down the hall toward the Dean of Students office.

As he entered the office waiting area, the secretary told him to go right in; the dean was expecting him. He entered the dean's office and saw Mar Janson, the biggest bully in his class, sitting in one of the chairs against the wall. The Dean told Caalin to have a seat. He then said, "Mr. Matthews, we just retrieved Mr. Janson's book bag from the top of the school's communications tower, and Mr. Janson is under the impression that you are the person who put it there." Caalin looked shocked as he tried to hold in his laughter.

"Dean Hawthorne, am I being held responsible for Marion's inability to keep track of his book bag?"

Mar gave Caalin an angry look. He didn't like to be called by his proper name. Mar was the biggest, meanest bully in school and picked on everyone. Caalin was the only person who was not afraid of him and loved to give him what he deserved—a taste of his own medicine.

The Dean's eyes were fixed on Caalin. "Mr. Matthews, this is the tenth time this month this has happened, and Mr. Janson has two witnesses that say they saw you put it on the tower."

"Sir, those witnesses are his buddies and would lie for him in an instant," Caalin calmly replied. "I could provide three people who would say I didn't put the bag there. Where did you say it was again?"

The Dean's face turned red as he pointed his finger into Caalin's face and, in a loud voice, declared, "MATTHEWS, I WILL BE WATCHING YOU, SO YOU BETTER TAKE THIS SCHOOL BREAK TO STRAIGHTEN YOURSELF OUT, NOW GET OUT OF MY OFFICE!"

As Caalin was leaving the office, he met his friends in the hall. They were running to get to the office to find out why Caalin was called in to see the Dean. As they got close, they heard a voice.

"Let's watch our speed in the halls, young men."

"Sorry, Ms. Chapman," the boys replied in unison.

When they reached Caalin, they quickly asked what had happened. Caalin was explaining what went on in the dean's office when Mar shouted at him. "This isn't the end of it, Matthews!"

Caalin replied, "Then bring it on, Marion!" Mar's face turned a deep red as he went in the other direction. Caalin and his friends exited the school laughing.

As they reached the area where the school's shuttles where waiting, Caalin told his friends he would see them later as they embarked for home. Once off the shuttle, he had been walking toward home for a few minutes when he looked up at Zartara and wondered if his father would bring the spaceship diagrams he had asked for. He then saw his father's shuttle coming into view and moving toward their home. Caalin broke into a run in hopes of getting there before him.

Caalin possessed an uncanny ability to run faster and jump higher than anyone else he knew. This is why he was able to put Marion's book bag at the top of the communications tower. Yes, Dean Hawthorne, he was the one that did it, but he was not going to admit to doing it if there was no proof of it. As Caalin ran, he recalled what he had been taught about how the world he called home became part of a set of planets grouped as one.

It was now over seventeen years and before he was born. Delron and Patora were two planets colonized by separate groups from Earth over three centuries before. At the time of the colonization of the planets, they were on opposite sides of the sun but in the same orbital path. Delron, with its six moons, and Patora, with its five moons, had slowly drifted toward each other over the last hundred years. As a result of the gravitational pull of both planets, they were on a collision course. As the two worlds grew closer together, scientists on both worlds worked to come up with a solution to the problem of the inevitable collision.

Both planets rotated in the same clockwise direction, so the scientists looked to the moons of each of the worlds for an answer to their problem. They soon discovered that of all the moons, Zatara, the largest moon of Delron, rotated in a counterclockwise direction, and its gravitational pull was negative to Delron's and Patora's positive. Zartara's gravity would pull on the Delron and Patora, but once they were close enough their gravity would push against each other. It would hold them in a group, allowing them to stay a safe distance from each other. The scientists calculated that if they could center the orbiting moon between the two planets at the precise time, the rotations of the three would lock like a set of gears and the gravity of Zatara would hold the planets at a safe distance from each other.

This would be a difficult task and timing was everything, so scientists from both planets worked together to build large stations on Zatara. They assembled massive rocket engines all around the moon's surface. These were to be used to maneuver the moon and change the direction of its movement as needed to correctly place it between the two worlds. Tunnels were created all through the moon, and a large spaceport was built inside. They blasted the smaller moons around the planets into smaller boulder-sized pieces to keep them from disrupting the maneuvering Zatara into position. It took the scientists and construction crews from both of the world's governments two years. With help from the planetary alliance and other worlds, they were able to complete it in that timeframe, as failure would mean the end of both worlds.

It took another year of studying and manipulation of the rockets and continuous blasting of the smaller moons, but finally Zatara was moving into place. As a precaution, most of the populations of both planets had earlier evacuated.

As Zatara moved into position, rockets were fired to impede any forward momentum and maneuver it into the correct location necessary to lock the group into position. Moments counted down as all systems and all efforts fell into place. The three planets locked into place, and then something strange happened.

Zatara had a small atmosphere that collided with Delron's and Patora's atmospheres. With a roar that rattled all three planets for about two hours, the three atmospheres finally formed into one surrounding the entire group. The new atmosphere made them look like one planet sliced into three sections.

Over the next two years, scientists blasted the moons around the planets until they formed an asteroid belt that circled the group. This created the only safe entryway to the new planetary group from either the north or south polar regions. It was determined that all incoming ships would enter from the southern polar region and exit to the northern polar region, allowing shipping traffic to and from the planet to flow safely. All ships would dock at the space dock on Zatara for inspection, and then be dispatched to their location on whichever planet they were bound for. Because of the newly formed atmosphere, open-shuttle vehicles could travel to and from the surfaces of all three planets with no problems.

Since a new planetary group now existed, the ruling families of both worlds joined together to set up a new government. They created a parliamentary system in which a member of each planet's ruling family would take a leadership position. A person elected by the combined population of the new alliance filled the third position in the leadership. The parliament headquarters was set up on the moon Zatara, as well as most of the government offices. A joint army and police force was formed, and parliament modified laws to meet the needs of the people of the newly formed planetary group. Each of the main planets functioned as they did before the merge. Solar power stations were built on Zatara to provide power for all the new government building. Water and food was provided by each of the other planets along with any other necessities.

The laws were the biggest hardship on the new alliance, but within the first year of the planetary creation, everything was completed. During the time of forming the new government, there were some outbreaks of violence, looting, and pirating, but the newly formed army and police forces, that were setup with help from the Planetary Alliance during the construction period, were able to handle everything that came up. Governmental offices and laboratories were also set up in Zatara to continue research and monitor the effects of gravitational shift. Customs offices were created to inspect cargo leaving and entering the planets.

One of the first issues faced by the new government was to name the new planetary group. After much deliberation and complicated referendum of the two worlds, the name Delpatara was selected and passed with a hundred percent of the votes in the parliament. Once the new government was firmly in place, the Planetary Alliance set up headquarters on Zatara and worked with the new government on diplomatic issues. New trade policies were developed with members of the Planetary Alliance now that the two worlds were one. The new government informed all the Planetary Alliance member planets of new regulations and policies for trading with the new planetary group. After all the hardships, the newly formed Delpatara and the new Planetary Alias headquarters were up and ready.

CHAPTER 2
Patora's Royal Family

During the last two years of the evacuation, the royal family from Patora set up a household on a smaller very heavy gravity planet called Doro-4. Its gravitational environment was 10 times that of Patora their home world. Everyone living on Doro-4 wore specialized equipment when outside the living quarters to counteract the gravitational pull of the planet. If not for the special devices the planet's gravity would crush them alive. Inside the living quarters, a computer system monitored and adjusted the planet's gravity automatically to maintain a comfortable gravitational environment.

During their stay on Doro-4, Lord Matthews shuttled between Zatara, their castle on Patora, and Doro-4 while overseeing the development of the new government. During their first year on Doro-4 Lady Matthews became pregnant and within nine months had a healthy baby boy they named Caalin. During his birth, solar flares from the sun sent out magnetic pulses causing problems with the computer systems that maintained the internal environment of the hospital. It seemed to be a minor glitch in the computer system, and did not last for very long so doctors were not concerned about any effect on the baby. However, no one knew what the real effects of the heavy gravity of Doro-4 would have since Caalin was the first child ever born in a gravity-adjusted environment. There had been children born on spaceships and space stations but that was a different type of environment. On spaceships and space stations environment are for creating gravity not reversing its effects.

It now has been a few years since the stabilization of the planets and the newly formed government was in place. Lord Matthews had moved the family back to the castle grounds they call Patora-Blade and he is now deeply involved with the new government of Delpatara. Caalin is almost six and is still adjusting to his life in this strange new world he now calls home. He was looking forward to all the adventures that were ahead of him or at least in his mind.

It seemed that because Caalin was born on a heavy-gravity planet his physical abilities far exceeded and are more advanced than those of his friends his age. He could climb higher, jump higher, lift more weight and run faster than any of his friends. His friends put him up to stealing barbar fruit (a crisp fruit that tastes like a cross between an apple and a fresh sweet peach). They would steal them from one of the local orchards. This was easy for Caalin; he could jump high enough to get the good ones at the top of the trees. He could also outrun and jump the dagaels (dog-like weasel animals the farmers use to guard their crops.) Reports of his troubles would eventually make their way back to Patora-Blade and Lady Matthews. She would quietly pay the farmer for his fruit and any damage that may have occurred so as not to worry Lord Matthews with little things.

A few years have gone by, the government is doing well and Lord Matthews has settled into his new ruling position with no issues. Caalin was still having minor problems with mischief. At school books and totes would find themselves in locations that no one could reach. Farmers' dagaels run until they dropped from exhaustion and fruit mysteriously disappears from treetops. This is the same type of mischief that had gotten him sent to the Dean's office this very day.

Caalin rounded the bend and saw his father's shuttle getting closer to home. He made a quick turn and through one of the orchards he ran. One of the farm's dagaels took chase but it did not take long before Caalin had left him in his dust. Today was Caalin's fourteenth birthday and he was hoping for some spaceship designs he had asked for.

Over the last year, he had been watching some of the older boys run skyracers (one-person rocket ships they built themselves). He had decided to build one of his own and race it himself. After weeks of scrounging parts here and there, he was ready to set out on his task of building his very own skyracer. First, he would need a set of plains. These were the plans he had hoped his father had brought him. His father also worked with the design board on new spaceship development so he would be able to get discarded plans.

Caalin reached the landing pad just as his father's shuttle touched down. He saw the large round tube under his father's arm and knew right away it was what he had asked for.

Caalin ran up to meet his father and eagerly asked, "Dad is that what I think it is?" Lord Matthews looks at him, "It is maps of the planet Cordonrue if that what you were thinking?" Caalin's jaw dropped and Lord Matthews laughed and handed him the tubes. "Yes they are the plans you were looking for, but don't completely cover your bedroom walls with them your mom will kill us both", he said with another laugh.

Later that night after a small party, that landed Caalin several gifts, he retired to his room and dug through the plans his father had given him. He searched through every plan until he found one called skip runner. It looked like a simple one-person rocket with some weird modifications so he decided these were the plans he would use. He modified the plans to look more like what he was envisioning before going to bed.

He was up bright and early the next day and immediately set out to work on his racer. After two weeks of hard work, he finally had the chassis and outer covering completed, with some help from his friends. Now he needed a power source that would work with his design.

A friend's father worked for the military shuttle pool and had some old engines in his maintenance bay that he was always tinkering on. They decided to ask him if they could look for parts they could use. When they arrive they were permitted to take anything they wanted from the old discarded parts in the salvage bay. Surveying the bay the group found what they thought would work in a small container in the back corner, an old engine that was small enough it would fit perfectly in Caalin's racer.

After two days of hard work, he and his friends had the engine in the skyracer, and now it was time to see if it would run. One of the first things he needed to do was a complete systems check.

Caalin had gotten an old military flight suit from a friend of his father and with some adjustments managed to get it to fit properly. He opened the hatch on the skyracer and sealed himself into the small compartment. First, checking all gages, fuel pressure levels, and finally firing up the engine. The skyracer slowly begins hovered about two meters above the ground as the engine was idling. He checked his energy readings on the engine to see if there were any leaks. He knew to check these things from all the manuals he had read repeatedly from the start of his project.

All systems seem to be a go, so Caalin decided his first run would be over the neighboring orchards. He gave the system a little throttle and slowly moved forward. He slowly pulled back on the lifter lever and slowly began to rise above the orchards. After an hour of soaring over the orchards, he returned to what he now called home base and immediately began to run more tests and system checks to make sure everything was ok. If everything checked out, he would give it the test of a lifetime tomorrow. After all the safety tests checked out, Caalin secured his skyracer in a tool shed, that was now his hanger.

That night his dreams were of racing through the sky and beating the older boys with their fancy racers. The next day he skipped breakfast, ran down to the hangar and pulled the racer out. He eagerly went through all the safety checks once again. As his friends slowly begin to arrive he told them about how the test run went the day before, while trying to decide who he would challenge for his first race.

After every test had been run Caalin used the racer to tow his friends on their skiffers (small surfboard crafts that only hover one to two meters above the ground) down to the fields used by the older kids to race their ships. Caalin quickly entered a couple of races with some of the younger teens, in which he was victorious. Later in the day, an older teen, about seventeen, challenged him to a race. Before knowing anything about where the course they would take, Caalin had accepted.

The older boy mapped out the race course; they would race to an asteroid sensor station on the edge of the atmosphere, circle it, and return to the finish line. Caalin had not flown his racer at that height, but he was not to be outdone. He intended to prove himself to the older boys, and thought his racer was up to the challenge. He rushed to get set up for the race and in doing so he skipped some of the safety checks. At the starting line Caalin could hear the starter shouted "on your march, set" and then the blast of an air horn and they were off.

The older boy took a quick lead with Caalin not far behind. In no time they were nearing the sensor station, and Caalin for the first time had taken the lead by a small margin. They were rounding the sensor when the older boy bumped Caalin's racer and sent it sideways into the sensor. There was a loud bang and a whistling sound in his racer. He had blown a pressure valve in the collision and his steering went out. His racer was now out of control and making a long slow spiral movement up through the outer atmosphere.

Luckily for Caalin, the bang into the sensor had set off alarms at a monitoring station on one of the lower asteroids just outside the atmosphere. The station commander immediately dispatched a cruiser to investigate and if necessary prevent the sensor from falling to the planet's surface and possibly killing anyone that might be in its path. The captain of the cruiser realizing what was happening and immediately locked a tractor beam onto Caalin's racer and towed it into the cruiser's shuttle bay.

Once onboard the cruiser Caalin was informed of his faith. He was now on his way to the Delpatara Police Station in Zatara. There his parents would be waiting along with charges of a minor operating an unregistered spacecraft, racing in a sensor field, and damaging a monitoring sensor. This was not going to be a pleasant ending for what seemed to have started as a great day.

Caalin slowly walked into the police station where his worried mother was waiting to greet him. His father was still in the magistrates' office and from what Caalin could see of him through the window he was extremely angry. Lord Matthews was just finding out for the first time all the mischief Caalin had been up to over the years including the ten times he had been called to the Dean of students in the past three months. After over an hour Lord Matthews joined the family, he had paid the fines, and Caalin's skyracer was confiscated, but that would not be the last of it. Lord Matthews said nothing to Caalin for the rest of the day.

CHAPTER 3

off to school

Later that evening after dinner Lady Matthews joined Lord Matthews in his library where they were still when Caalin retired to bed. The next morning over breakfast the silence between Caalin and his father was finally broken by Lord Matthews informed him that he had two days to tell his friend goodbye. Caalin was shocked, and quickly questioned why. His father told him that he would be leaving for Boldoron Academy for the rest of his schooling. Caalin was not happy with his father's decision, and every night he would try to persuade him to change his mind, but this was to no avail and the two day flew by fast.

Caalin said goodbye to all his friends and was now boarding the family shuttle. They would travel from Patora-Blade to the spaceport on Zatara, from there to the space station Gama-12. At Gama-12 he would catch the school shuttle to the Academy. The flight seemed to have taken forever but they were now at Gama-12. He did not have a lot of time to look around the space station as the school shuttle was already there waiting for him when he arrived. The shuttle was ready to depart from gate delta-3 so his parent had to say goodbye to him at the airlock.

Caalin's mother cried as she said good-bye to him and his father told him that this was for his own good. He told Caalin the Academy would help him find himself and give him some direction in his life. Both his parents stood waving good-bye until the airlock doors close, then they made their way back to their shuttle.

Once inside the shuttle Caalin begin to check out the other occupants. As he looked around the shuttle he saw a boy and girl both with green skin and wearing gold and royal blue full length traveling coats. The boy was the same height as Caalin; he was green with lighter green hair, he had teal green eyes and was rather handsome. The girl, who was a little shorter, had dark green hair and the same teal green eyes and was very good looking as well.

Across the shuttle from Caalin sat a beautiful young girl. She was slender and a little shorter than Caalin. She had snow-white hair with a tint of light morning blue in it, her eyes were a bright grey blue and to his surprise she had snowy white wings. He saw her stretch them, and they look as if they reached two meters across or maybe more. She was wearing a shirt that fit around her wings and did not come all the way down to the pants she was wearing. Sitting next to her was a smaller boy that looked to be about four and a half feet tall, with mousy brown hair, brown eyes and ears that seem to be a little large for his head. He was wearing what look like a poly fiber suit of armor. Caalin though he heard the girl call the boy her cousin, but they did not look anything alike plus the boy did not have wings. The others in the shuttle also eyed Caalin who was now five foot four inches tall, with his straw yellow blonde uncombed hair and bright blue eyes. They all watched each other to see who would be the first to start a conversation. After a few minutes of silence the cabin doors opened and in walked a tall figure dressed in a royal blue uniform with crimson red piping. His skin was a brilliant orange color, his eyes were black and his hair, which came down below his shoulders, and his mustache that dropped about three inches off his face, were a deep dark green. "hello young ladies and gentlemen" he said, "I'm professor Taran, I will be your councilor at the school, so if you have any problem or question please feel free to come see me. Once we reach the school an escort will show you to your dorm. You will store your personal items and then follow your escort to the dining hall for dinner. At dinner you will meet the rest of the freshman class and the staff. You will get your class assignment for your first semester after dinner. I regret inform you that first year students at the academy have their classes assigned for them. We assign basic classes to everyone and after the first year you will be allowed to select your own classes."

He continued, "Since you will have about two hours before we reach the school you can spend the time designing your group logo. This will designate your individual group in the squadron and will give you a since of belonging. I have some photos here of plants and animals from many different planets. You may select one of them to go on your group logo or you may come up with your own design, it does not have to be a plant or animal. You will also need to select a name for the group that will also go on your uniforms. Mr. Matthews, I have been told you are somewhat of an artist, and from the drawing of the skyracers you have brought with you, I would agree. You will draw the logo out the best you can and turn it into me before we leave the shuttle. I will have the logo made up and sewn on you uniforms. I will leave you on your own for now and will see you again once we have docked at the school." He handed the photos to Caalin turned and exited through the same door he had entered from earlier.

Caalin took the photos and moved to a table that was in the center of the room. The others slowly begin to join him as he spread the photos out on the table. He looked up at everyone as they took their seats, "It looks like we have some decisions to make so I think it would be a good idea if we introduce ourselves. My name is Caalin Matthews; I'm form the planet group Delpatara, the planet of Patora." Then the tall green boy said, "I'm Ssamuel Ssallazz, my friends call me Ssam and this is my sister." The girl quickly interrupted him, "I can introduce myself thank you very much! I'm Ssophia Ssallazz and we are from Greckonia." Ssam leaned in and whispered, "Don't ever call her Sophie she hates that name." Ssophia then smacked him in the back of the head and told the group that she just preferred people call her by her proper name.

Next the young girl with the beautiful wings spoke, "I am Angiliana Avora you can call me Ang and this is my cousin and best friend Mortomous Valtor but we call him Mouse." She was pointing at the smaller boy in a poly-carbon outfit that almost looked like armor. He just nodded his head and took his seat at the table.

"Well" said Caalin "it seems we need to pick out something to go on our group logo, so dig in everyone" and with that everyone set down at the table and begin looking at the photos. There were strange rhinoceros looking creature with wings, plants with claws and teeth, insect the look like small elephants and miniature dragons.

Ang picked up a picture a blue Bangalor Dragon bursting through a ball of fire and smoke, trying to look as fierce as possible for something so small. Bangalor Dragons only grow to twelve to fourteen inches in height and try to look fierce when they feel threatened. "I like this one" she stated and everyone leaned over to look. Ssophia look at the picture then said to Ssam "that could be our cousin Zearn". Ssam laughed and said, "Looks a lot like him" then the entire group laughed. They all decided they like the dragon picture for the logo and Caalin set out drawing up some ideas. The boys remained at the table talking about what changes to make, what colors to use, and how fierce the dragon should look.

The girls just moved to the side and began discussed boys in general. After about thirty minutes had past the captain came over the intercom and stated that they had early clearance to depart Gama-12 and would be pulling away now, they would be arriving at the school within the hour.

Caalin had finished the drawing now and was showing it to everyone for their approval. The logo was a round ball of flames with a fierce looking Bangalor Dragon bursting through the flames. It was encircled in a ring and below the dragon was the name BANGALORS. Caalin looked at everyone and said, "We may as well call ourselves Bangalors if we are going to use one on our logo." Everyone quickly agreed and told Caalin what a good drawing it was.

The ship uncoupled from Gama-12, and slowly made a turn away from the station, then began to move forward. Once it was five kilometers out Caalin could see what looked like lighting beginning to emit from the front of the ship. There was a loud crackle, a blue flash and then a jerk. Everyone move to the windows to see what was happening. Gama-12 was now gone and the stars around them looked nothing like the ones that were there before. Then there was a small voice saying "Dimensional jump engines, that is what they have" it was Mouse. "They are able to use them to jump from one point in space to another faster than the speed of light; we could be light years from Gama-12 by now." He continued. Everyone continued to look out into space and could see a cat's eye nebula coming up. "That's where the school is," said Ang "there is only one planet inside the nebula and the school is the only thing on the planet. They say that only the members of the staff can safely guide ships through the nebula to the school."

CHAPTER 4

The Academy

Moments later Professor Taran's voice came over the intercom," Students please gather up all the material I gave you and prepare for landing. We will be at the school in twenty minutes; I will see you once we've landed." Everyone moved back to the Table and gathered up all the pictures and papers. Caalin took them, put them in a neat stack, and place their logo drawing on the top. Once the ship had landed Professor Taran return and Caalin quickly gave him the stack of papers and pointed out their logo on top. "Very good" stated the professor as he led them through the airlock, the docking bay. As they entered the docking bay they had to walk through a scanned that scanned their measurements for their school uniforms. After they were scanned they moved into the hallways of the school itself.

Inside the halls of the school, they met a tall grey blue looking lad with fixed black eyes. Professor Taran quickly introduced him "students this is Ra, he is one of the upper classmen; he will be showing you to your dorm." "You will store all your personal items and then Ra will escort you to dining hall. I will see you at dinner," he concluded. With that he went in one direction as Ra led them in the other.

They entered a hallway with rolls of doors running down both sides, "this is the Alpha wing" announced Ra "you're in Alpha twelve." They stopped in front of a door marked A-12 and Ra opened the door to a large common room. Inside a large table set in the middle with several chairs around it. On one side of the room were three computer workstations with holographic monitors, on the opposite wall was a large bookcase full of books. The back wall had two doors one mark boys and the other girls. In the girl's room, there were two beds and four cabinets, two for each girl. In the back of the room was the door that leads to the girl's showers. The boy's room was set up similar but for three people instead of two.

Everyone's luggage had already been placed in the rooms. Ra turned to face saying, "Please put your thing away, I'll return in thirty minutes to escort you to the dining hall. You may put up photos and posters to make your area feel more like home if you wish."

They unpacked their luggage and placed their things in the cabinets. Caalin pull out some of his skyracer and starship posters and put them on the wall over his bed, trying to make it look as close as he could to his room back home. Ssam and Mouse stopped what they were doing long enough to admire some of the art work, and then completed their unpacking.

The group was sitting in the large common room when Ra returned to lead them to the dining hall. They exited the door turning right then walking down the long hallway until reaching an adjoining hall and turning right again. They made their way down this hall passing more hallways leading in both directions that were identical to the hallway their room was on. The only difference was the color of the walls. The wall color in their hallway was a crimson red the others were royal blue, gold and green.

They soon entered a larger round room with a huge glass dome overhead and on one of the walls hung a large shield. Behind the shield a large sword was position so it went straight down the middle. On the shield, these words formed a ring, *Per Scientia Adveho Vires, Per Vires Adveho Pacis, Per Pacis Adveho Scientia*. In the center of the ring it read, *Sic Est Orbis of Vita*. "This is the central commons area." Ra stated as they turned left and continued walking.

They entered another hallway with several double doors down both sides and at the end a large set of double doors. Walking through the doors at the end of the hall they entered the large dining room. Several long tables ran the length of the room in the colors of crimson red, royal blue, gold and dark green. Above the red table was a banner for Alpha

Squadron. Over the blue it was Beta, the gold was Charlie and the green was Delta. At the far end of the Tables were four large tables running the width or the room with strips of the same four colors running down the middle. "Newbie's set at the front, you have a designated table at the far end," stated Ra, "you will find your names on your seats"

They slowly made their way down to the end of the tables with all the older students staring and whispering as they passed. Quickly finding their sits they set down in hopes of cutting down the stares. As they looked around, they noticed that each of the other groups had also received five new students. This meant there were twenty newbie's at the school, maybe this would take some of the pressure off them.

Caalin looked at the tables on the end but there was no one seated at them, then Ra appeared through the door next to the tables and shouted "All Rise." Everyone stood up as the school staff walked through the door. They moved down the tables until all were standing behind a seat, then at the same time they took their seats. Ra shouted, "Be seated" and everyone sat down again.

The tall man in the middle stood up and addressed the students "Good evening students for those of you who don't know, I am Headmaster Keayan, and I would like to take this time to welcome all the new students to Boldoron Academy." He concluded with, "You will find when you return to your dorms your uniforms and class schedules will be there waiting for you." Breakfast is at six o'clock and classes will begin at eight, now enjoy your dinner." After that he set down in his seat and began to eating and talking with the staff.

Dinner was different for almost everyone, since the students were from different worlds the food was prepare to meet each individuals needs. Some of the things served seemed to be still alive and some looked like insect. There were items with tentacles that were moving and some things were trying to craw away. Although it was strange to see the different foods Caalin and his new friends were still able to enjoy their meals.

After dinner, the group made their way back to the dorm room, making a few wrong turns, having to back track a few times, and finally asking an upper classman for directions. When they entered, the room setting on the large table was stacks of uniforms, books, small handheld computers, and their class schedules.

The uniforms were metallic gray, with crimson red shoulder epilates. On the left sleeve was the patch that they had designed on the flight in, a Bangalor dragon bursting through the flames, and the name BANGLORS below it. The patch looked a lot better than the original picture. On the right sleeve was a large A for Alpha squadron. Over the right vest pocket was the words Alpha Squadron and over the left pocket was their last names. The uniforms were designed specifically to fit each of them perfectly. Even Ang's was tailored to fit around her wings.

Everyone set down to look at the schedules, and the first thing they noticed was all their classes were the same; they would be attending them as a group. At eight o'clock, they had Universal History, nine o'clock Engineering, eleven o'clock self-defense, and from twelve o'clock until one thirty they lunch. After lunch at one thirty was Universal Art, and then two thirty class Universal Botany. Finally, the last class for the day Universal Geology from three thirty to four thirty. They would have a half hour of free time before dinner at five, which allowed them time to put away any books and freshen up for dinner.

It was now getting late so everyone decided to retired for the evening and scurried off to the bedrooms. The boys were having a hard time sleeping so Mouse and Ssam were questioning Caalin about his home world. Caalin was explaining that he had not actually been born on his home planet, that he was born on Doro-4. He told them about how the scientist of Delron and Patora had worked together to save the planets from impending doom. He also filled them in on how he would raid the fruit orchards and run the dagaels until they dropped. He finally told them about the skyracer he had built and the race that got him in so much trouble his parent decided to send him here to give him some direction in life.

Next Ssam told them about his home planet, how it had beautiful forests, large fresh water oceans and about the different animals that lived on the planet. How he and his sister were constantly fighting with each other, which was one the reasons they were at the academy. Ssam was also getting them into trouble at school. Their parents thought it would help them mature, as they put it.

Mouse laughed at Ssam story, and then told them about his home planet of Averiaera. Not all the people that lived on the planet have wings but Ang could explain that better than he could. Ang's parents were part of the ruling family of the House of Avora and they lived in the cliff city high in the mountains. Mouse's father was a member of the royal family Valtor and his mother was Ang's aunt.

Ang and he were not only cousins but also best friends and they did almost everything together. He had modified a skiffer so it would fly higher than any others and Ang would tow him through the city using a rope. They would race through mountain canyons and the city streets, with her flying and him in tow. Both their parents though that they were getting to reckless with their actions so that is why they were at the school.

Ssam asked what a skiffer was and Mouse explained it was a small hover board that you stood on and once you got it started you could move it in any direction you wanted to travel. The stories finally came to a stopped and the boys slowly drifted off to sleep.

CHAPTER 5

classes begin

The next morning the boys met the girls in the common room and went to the dining hall together for breakfast. At breakfast, the boys filled the girls in on their discussion from the night before going into detail about Caalin's skyracer and the race that got him sent to the academy. The girls seemed to be interested in the race especially Ang, who was looking at Caalin very intently making him a little uncomfortable for some reason. He went over all the details of the race and how his skyracer was confiscated, by the time he finish the story breakfast was over. After breakfast, they made their way down the halls looking for the Universal History classroom. Ang quickly stopped an upper-classmate girl and asked for direction, she pointed them back down the hall and to the right. As they started back down the hall Ang turned to Ssophia and said, "Boys, never want to ask for directions they think they always know where they are going!" Ssophia let out a loud laugh and then Ang joined in but the boys just gave them an angry look.

When they reached the classroom, the five new Delta squadron students were already there. The Delta's uniforms were grey with green shoulders, had a large D on the right sleeve and their logo on the left. Their logo looks like a large winged serpent, swallowing someone whole, in a circle of blood with the name Algeron below it. Algeron was the name of the mythical serpent of the planet Petaya. Half the population of Petaya disappeared over a century ago and it was said that Algeron came down from the skies and swallowed them all alive.

The delta group gave them an evil stare as they took their seats. The Deltas was also made up of three boys and two girls like Alpha group. One of the boys, whose name on his uniform was Drake, seemed to be the leader of the group as he was bossing the others around. He had light grey colored skin, mud brown hair, and reddish eyes that seem to glow when the light hit them at the right angle. There was one cute girl with blue skin, blood red hair that reached her shoulders and bright yellow eyes, her nametag said Peetora. Another boy was blue, with blue hair and almost glowing silver colored eyes, his tag said Cizin. The third boy was huge and broad at the shoulders, his hair was a grayish blue, skin a darker blue and eyes were dark brown, his nametag said Ah Puch. Then the final one in the group was another attractive girl who looked like she could be related to Ssam and Ssophia. Her skin was green, with long dark green hair and bright green eyes, her nametag said Vale.

Before anyone had time to say anything to each other, Professor Taran walked in wearing the same type uniform as the Alpha students. He looked up at the class," Please, be seated." He then proceeded to call roll. He went down the name of the Alpha group then the Delta group. He called out the Delta Squad names; they were Dargon Drake, Devlon Ah Puch, Jon Cizin, Evalon Peetora and Keyan Vale. Then he said, "Open your books to the first chapter on Planetary and Non Planetary Alliance Planets", and continued, "It is important that you know the difference in the two groups." "Mr. Matthews this is part of your family history, your great grandfather's father led the movement to establish the Planetary Alliance," Taran said, as there was a snarl from the delta group. "The Planetary Alliance is made up of all the planets that have signed a non aggression and trade treaty with each other" He stated "the Non Alliance planets refused to join, and are believed to be safe havens for pirates and criminals." Dargon spoke up, "You will have a hard time proving that sir." The professor looked over at him and said, "You are right for the non alliance planets are good at hiding what they do, am I not correct Mr. Drake?" Dargon just sneered at the professor.

The professor continued, "You will find out that the Delta Squadron is made up completely of individuals from the Non Alliance Planets. Their parents prefer that they be separated from any influence of the Alliance." "Now I would like you to write a short essay on the creation of the Alliance, it founders and those planets that did not join. I would also like you to explain the reasons why they joined or did not join. You may work on it for the rest of the class period and it has to be turned in tomorrow", after saying that the professor set down and begin going over some papers on his desk. The class began reading their books on the planetary alliance and jotting down notes.

After what seemed like forever, the bell rang and everyone rose from their seats and started off to their next class. Dargon made it a point to run into Caalin and call him alliance scum as the Delta group went out the door cutting off Caalin and the others. Mouse tried to dart past Caalin to say something but Ang grabbed him by the collar and pulled him back, saying, "This is not the time or place." Then the professor looked up from his desk and said, "She is right Mr.Valtor, you will get your chance in the skyracer race." Caalin looked at the professor and quickly asked "What are you talking about sir." Professor Taran answered, "You'll find out later, now get along to your next class." With that, they all left in search of the engineering class still wondering what the Professor's comment was all about.

They soon found the engineering classroom, where they met the Beta group's new students. The Beta students were an average looking group made up of two boys and three girls and did not look or act anything like the Deltas. Their uniforms were just like the other groups except the shoulders were blue and they had a large B on the right one. Their logo was a comet on a midnight blue background and the word Ice Comets below it. They quickly introduce themselves to the Alpha group.

Professor Marru came in wearing the uniform that Charlie Squadron wore, his skin was almost grey, and his hair was black and oily looking. His brown eyes seem to be the only color in his face. He took a quick roll call and then told the students, "You will now go through these doors" he turned and pointed to a set of double doors that were right behind him. "Once you are in the shop area you will find a work area all ready marked with your squadron's identification" he continued, "you will spend this semester building a skyracer, at the end of the semester there will be a race between each squadron to see who has built the best racer." "You will find manuals and different plans that you can use or if you choose you can design your own. I will be available for any technical help if you have any questions and will be performing safety checks to make sure your systems are safe to operate." he concluded by saying, "If you have no questions then move to your areas and start your work." After that he move to the back of the shop, set down at a desk, and started looking at what looked like design plans for some type of plasma engine.

Caalin was thrilled, he had no idea that he would get to build another skyracer. He quickly moved over to their area grabbed the stack of plans from the workbench and started looking them over. Mouse and Ssam ran to catch up but the girls took their time to join the boys. As they looked over the plans, the boys would comment about what they liked or did not like on each of the plan. Caalin looked at them and said, "You remember what the professor said, we can design our own, we can use what we like about each of these to design one the way we want." With that said, they started highlighting the things they like on each of the plans, trying to figure out what would work with what as they went through them.

Caalin and Mouse got a blank sheet of paper and started drafting out what they were going to do. The girls moved over to their parts bin and started sorting out the different parts to make it easier to locate what they needed. This also allowed them the opportunity to talk about the boys in the Beta Squad. Ssam went through the plans and began making a list of parts they would need for the racer, starting with engine parts.

By the end of the two-hour class, the girls had the parts sorted, and the boys had most of the new design ideas down on paper. Professor Marru informed them they could take the plans with them and work on later if they wished. Caalin quickly rolled up the plans while Ang got a tube from the professor to put them in. As they were leaving the room they looked over at the Beta groups work area, the Beta group had selected a plan from their stack and had already started building their engine.

The next class was self-defense which was also with Beta squadron. The classroom was easy to find, it was just down the hall from the engineering classroom. They entered the room to find Professor Kai already there and waiting. She was about five feet six inches tall with short purple hair and dark blue eyes and very attractive and wearing the Beta squadron uniform. As they walked in she announced, "Alpha down the left side of the mats,

Beta down the right, please." They did as she asked and turned facing the mats. "Today I will teach you some basic moves to block an attacker from making contact with your body," she said. She selected the largest boy in the group, who happened to be in the Beta group, to help her demonstrate the moves. She showed everyone three basic blocking techniques and then paired them for practice, and of course she paired Caalin with the largest boy. She would have Beta be the attacker for a few minutes then switch and Alpha would be the attackers. This went on for the entire class period until she thought they knew the moves perfectly. As they were getting ready to leave the class, she assigned the some moves in their textbooks to practice that evening, telling everyone they would go over them in class the next day.

They made their way from the classroom and back toward the dining hall for lunch. They talked with the Beta group about the moves as they walk and scheduled a time to meet them in the common hall to practice them. At lunch, the boy's conversation went back to discussing the plans for their racer, while the girls discussed one of the cute boys in the Beta group. During their conversations, Professor Kai came walking by on her way to the instructor tables. Ang quickly stopped her and ask, "Professor would it alright if we use your classroom this evening to practice our moves with Beta group." The professor told her that would be fine, that she may even stop by to check on them if they didn't mind. Ang quickly answered, "That would be great professor; thank you." Professor Kai then turned and continued on to her table to enjoy her lunch. This gave Ang and Ssophia a good reason to go over to the Beta table and let the others know, plus get another close look at the cute boy again. They giggled as they got up from the table and started over to the Beta table. Caalin and Mouse looked up at them, then at each other, shook their heads and went back to their conversation about the racer.

As lunch ended, the girls rejoined the boys, gathered their books and they all trotted down the hall to their Universal Art class. This was a class they shared with Charlie squadron, who like Beta had two boys and three girls and where also more average looking than the Delta squad. Their uniforms had gold shoulders and they logo was a white winged horse with flames coming from its nostrils with the name Dragon Stallions below it. The groups hit it off with each other right away; Charlie group asked them what they thought of the Deltas. By this time Charlie squad had endured two classes with them, one of which was self-defense. The Delta's were so rough that Professor Kai had to reprimand them several times. The girls showed them some bruises they had gotten during the practice. Ang told them, "We are going to be practicing our self-defense moves with Beta group later this evening and would be honored to have Charlie group join us." The Charlie group quickly accepted the offer, they could use the practice, and they wanted to be ready for the Deltas the next day.

At that time, Professor Fisatoria entered the room, wearing a multicolored dress; she was a tall attractive woman, with multicolored hair and her eyes seem to constantly change color. One moment they are blue, then green, then grey, and then brown. She considered herself a free spirit and seemed to float as she walked. She was the first instructor they had met that did not wear a uniform. She asked the students to take their seats. She informed, "Today they will be looking at Antorian and Boranian Art and how they are similar in some ways and different in others." She asked everyone to turn to page ten in the text. She then walked over and began putting pictures up on the wall for everyone to see. Each picture had a number on it and she asked them, "Would you please take out your computers and go to the Arts115 program, you will find these same pictures. I would like you to use your text book to look up the characteristics for each of the pictures. I then would like for you to tell me if they are Antorian or Boranian." She continued with, "at the end of the class we will download your answers and tomorrow I will let you know how well you did." "This is just to give me an idea of where we stand concerning your knowledge of art" she finished with, "please get started." The students flipped back and forward from page to page, reading about the difference in the two art styles, marking the pictures in the computer Antorian or Boranian. At the end of class they transmitted, their answers to Professor Fisatoria's computer and trotted off to their next class. As they left, the room the Charlie squad shouted they would see them later.

For their next class they had to go back through the commons area, down another long hallway, and through a door that opened into a large glass dome filled with all kinds of plants. In the middle of the dome was a classroom that also made completely of glass. They could see Professor Ravin, who wore a Delta squad uniform; he was a tall blue skin man with no hair and eyes that were deep dark red. He was seating at a large table with some weird plants on it. As they neared, the room the Delta squadron came in behind them and the Alphas could hear the snide remarks that Dargon was making about Caalin. He boasted, "There is Mr. Planetary Alliance himself, thinks he's famous, I need to show him famous" by this time Caalin had turned around to face him but Mouse and Ssam grabbed his arms and said the professor can see us, and pulled him toward the classroom. Dargon laughed, "Good thing they saved you Matthews." The rest of his group joined him in laughter.

They entered the classroom and Professor Ravin looked up at them then turned and looked at the Delta group, "You think you're amusing don't you Mister Drake? This is neither the time nor place for comments like that; now please take your seats." They all sat down, Dargon now had an angry look on his face. Caalin was wondering how the professor heard the comments, did he have super hearing? The professor then said, "take out you computers, click on Botany199, you will find these fifteen planet, using your textbooks, you will identify each plant, its planet of origin and how it is most commonly used. At the end of this period you will transmit your results to me and I will let you know how well you have done tomorrow."

Again everyone went to work looking through the text trying to locate the plants, where they came from and what they were most commonly used for. This was harder than it looked; many planets that look alike. You had to look closely at the leaves, the number of leave, the size of the stems and the type of flower, if they had any. Everyone was glad when the class was over and they had transmitted the results to the professor. Alpha had made it a point to transmit theirs and leave before the Deltas had a chance to catch up.

Their next class was Universal Geology as they reached the room Charlie group was already there. They greeted each other and Ssophia begin telling the girls everything that had happened with Delta. She told them about the comments that Dargon had made and how Caalin almost started a fight with him. As they all took their seat professor Grundor walked in, and all fell silent, he was one of the strangest look of the instructors with no hair on his head, his skin was green and brown. He almost looked to be made of rock, his eyes were a deep green in color and he was extremely shorter than all the other instructors.

They all seat quietly waiting to see what he had in store for them. His uniform was not like that of any of the students it was grey with orange shoulders. This class went just like the last two, and was what Caalin considered the boringness class so far. He had them go to their computer and their textbooks and determent to origin of twenty different rock samples he had on his desk. They would take the rocks, examine them, and pass them around to each other. Then they would flip back and forward in their textbook and then input their findings into the computer. "It is like all the instructors are using the same study plan," Caalin murmured. He suddenly received a kick under the table from Ang, to go along with the angry look she had on her face. At the end of class, they transmitted the information and left the classroom, telling the other group they would see them later.

CHAPTER 6

Building the skyracer

It was too early for dinner so the group made their way back to their dorm room. There the boys took the opportunity to spread out their racer plans and go over a few more modifications they had discussed earlier. The girls decided to set down and look over the new self-defense moves, as they wanted to impress the cute boys they had met in both Beta and Charlie squadrons. After about thirty minutes they made their way back to the dining hall.

At dinner, Ssophia and Ang moved from table to table talking to the girls of Beta and Charlie squads and doing a little flirting with the boys. A few of the boys from Beta made their way over to talk with Caalin, Mouse and Ssam about their racer and to compare designs. Caalin only showed them what Alpha's design looked like but not the engine design; it was going to be their secret.

After dinner, the groups went back to their dorms to let their food settle before going to self-defense practice. Once in the dorm the girls disappeared to their room and the boys went over to one of the computers and began going through the designs for the racer. They were able to pull up the designs they were using from the engineering database. They then pull from each of the designs the different items they wanted to use and created a master file with all the items for their design. Mouse was great at doing all the computer work and quickly had all the designs they wanted in just a matter of minutes. The holographic computer system was great it allowed them to move parts around to see where they would best fit in a three dimensional display. This allowed them to turn the design in any direction they wanted so they could see all the connections they need to make.

They were able see how the parts would fit together or if they fit the design at all. They decided to start with the engine to make sure it would work, and then build the frame around it. They took several parts from different engines, but some had to be discarded as failures and others that worked were added to the parts list. After working on the design for an hour the girls reappeared. Ang commented, "We need to be leaving to meet the other groups." The boys save their file and followed the girls out the door and down the hall.

The five of them arrived at the self-defense classroom just at the same time as the others. One of the boys from Beta squad opened the door and everyone entered the classroom. As they walked in Professor Kai came out of her office to greet them. She announce, "I took the liberty to invite the Delta squadron to join you, but it looks like they think they don't need the extra training. I am proud of you all for wanting to come by and practice. It shows me you really care about learning how to defend yourselves." Everyone thanked Professor Kai for letting them use the classroom and was relieved Delta squad decided not to attend, none of the group wanted to deal with anyone from Delta. Professor Kai continued, "I will just set at my desk and observe, if anyone had any questions or needed any help I will be happy to assist."

Everyone paired off with books at their sides and began trying one move after another. Each would tell the other how their move was or what they thought was wrong with it. Professor Kai would giggle a little when someone's attempt at a move that did not go as planned. Nevertheless, she did not correct them or say anything about the move. After two hours of practice she stood up, "it is getting late and you should be getting back to your dorms, I will see you in class tomorrow. She then turned and went back into her office. The groups picked up their books and made their way out the door and back down the halls toward their dorms.

While practicing, everyone had the opportunity to talk with each other about their home planets and families. Through their discussion, they had found they all had one thing in common. They were all members of ruling families, and they were here to mainly to learn discipline, diplomacy and to build their character or that was what their parents had continuously told them. Everyone wondered what kind of ruling family the Delta squad students came from, supposedly they were from non alliance planets that were part of the pirating issues the Alliance had to deal with in the past.

It was late when they got back to their rooms, but the boys wanted to work on their racer a little more, so the girls went to their room to study leaving the boys at the computer, The boys made some modifications to their engine design based one of the Charlie student's suggestions and it worked great. Some of the parts that did not work before fit perfectly into place. They brought the engine up on the holographic computer and ran it through a simulation to test it; everything worked with no problems. All the safety checks and stress tests on the engine simulator, tested out positive in the simulations. The boys went to their room happy, knowing their engine would worked fine. Once in the room out came the Universal History books and they started skimming the material they were assigned to read. Not really reading it but just the highlights that they thought they would see on the quiz.

The next day over breakfast, the boys caught Ang and Ssophia up on the changes they had made on the engine, and how all the test on the computer simulator came out great. The girls were not impressed and kept watching the boys in the other groups, and checking out the all older boys in the squadrons. After breakfast, they made their way to the universal history classroom, arriving at the same time as the delta group and the remarks started coming from Dargon the minute he saw them. "Oh look it is Lord Caalin of the great planetary alliance," he started, but before he could continue the professor walked up. He immediately told them to take their seats and began class by handing out a test on the material he had assigned them to read. Everyone struggled through the test, everyone except Ang and Ssophia. They had actually read the material, where Caalin, Mouse and Ssam had only read what they thought was important. Unfortunately, the questions wanted more details than the boys had read. After the test Professor Taran went over the material he had assigned the night before, as he did Caalin recounted his answers on the test trying to count the number of questions he had correct. By the time, they had completed going over the material it was the end of class and they had another reading assigned for the next day.

They hurried to the engineering class, the boys were eager to get started on the racer. The girls came along slowly, not as eager as the boys to get started. Once in class they started going back through the parts separating them in to different groups according to Ssam's new parts list. The girls volunteered to do this, to the delight of the boys, but mainly because it gave them the opportunity to talk with the others as they took parts back to the bins and picked up new ones. This left the boys free to start building the engine for the racer. They pulled out their engine plans and started grabbing parts listed on the specification list. Once they had all the parts, they began piecing them together. Marty, one of the Beta boys came over to borrow a spanner wrench, but really wanted to see how things were going, and to his surprise, the engine was starting to come together very nicely. By the end of class, the girls had all the parts sorted and the boys had the engine almost complete, so they covered everything with a canvas tarp and headed out for the next class.

Self-defense class went well the moves they had practiced the night before were a lot easier to do. At the end of class the professor had not assigned any new moves for everyone to practice that night, so after class they rushed off to lunch. After lunch they met their friends in Charlie group at arts class, the boys started talking about how well their engine was coming along. The girls however were discussing how awful the Delta group was during their other classes. They were telling Ang and Ssophia all the bad things Dargon had said about Caalin. In Art class everything went well, they discussed the fine art of Mordonru and before class was over Professor Fisatoria told them they would begin drawing the next day.

They left class telling the other group they would see them later in Geology. Then made their way to Botany class and as they arrived, the Delta group was already at the door. Dargon was standing there with a smirk on his face as usually and as Caalin walked pass he made the comment, "Does your girls always hold you back from fights, Lord Caalin dear?" Caalin turn grab Dargon and threw him sending him about six meters across the room, this was a move they had been practicing in self-defense class. Jon and Devolon grabbed Caalin as Dargon quickly got up and charge toward him, but he was tripped by Ssophia and crashed into Devolon knocking him to the floor. Caalin quickly threw Jon further than he had thrown Dargon. By this time, Professor Ravin was at the door and quickly stopped the mayhem. He marched everyone into the classroom and had everyone take their seats. He went to his desk, took out a pad and pen wrote something on two sheets of the paper. He then walked over and gave one to Caalin and the other to Dargon. "You will both report to the headmaster's office this evening after dinner" he stated. Dargon gave Caalin an evil look as Professor Ravin went back to his desk. He then passed out a sheet with fifty plants on it for them to identify and tell what their uses were. Jon's head throbbed from his landing he took after Caalin threw him which made concentrating on the work sheet more difficult. Eventually the class was over with no extra assignments and they made their way out the door before the Delta group could even get out of their seats.

They met the Charlie group in the hall on the way to Geology and quickly filled them in on what had happen. How Caalin had thrown both Dargon and Jon and how Ssophia had trip Dargon causing him to crash into Devolon. They all laughed at the picture in their minds of the two of them flying through the air and the looks on their faces. Everyone went completely quite when they heard that Caalin had to go see the headmaster after dinner.

They all entered the classroom and took their seats; the girls were all staring and smiling at Caalin now, as if to admire him for his courage to take on the Delta boys. Professor Grundor quickly passed out containers with rocks in them. They had to identify and labeled, but before he took his seat, he turned to the class to tell them that it will make up half of their course grade. They went through all the samples and painstakingly looked them up for identification. Soon class was over and they now have some free time before dinner. Both groups went to the main common area where they met up with Beta group. Once they were all together they continued the talk about the encounter with Delta outside of the Botany class. Everyone laughed about how the Delta boys didn't have a chance to do anything before they were bouncing off the wall. Caalin had gotten the best of them, but as everyone talked Caalin set quietly wondering what the headmaster would have in store for him.

At dinner, Caalin found he did not have much of an appetite with his meeting with the headmaster coming up. He picked at his food until he finally had enough and left for the headmaster's office. Everyone wished him good luck as he walked by, but he was not paying attention and just made his way out the door and down the hall.

CHAPTER 7

Detention

Caalin made his way down one hall after another until he reached the main office. He entered the office and was met by both Ms Serinora and Ms Teletora. They smiled at him and told him to have a seat. Soon Ms Platoron appeared from the Headmasters office with a not so happy Dargon in tow. She escorted him out the door and sent him on his way back to his dorm. She then turned to Caalin and said, "Follow me please Mr. Matthews" as she walked back into the office. Caalin slowly rose from the chair and followed her into the room.

Headmaster Keayan was looking out the window behind his desk with his back to the door as Caalin walked in. "Please have a seat Mr. Matthews," he said as he slowly turned to face Caalin. He had a stern look on his face as he took his seat behind the desk. "Mr. Matthews I went to school here at this very academy with your father and Mr. Drake's father," he paused for a second, "they too did not get along at first and found themselves doing a number of detentions together. Rules are rules Mr. Matthews and we cannot have students fighting in the hallways or classrooms." "You and Mr. Drake will server detention with Professor Grundor for a full week; he has some large geological samples that need to be broken down to be used in his classes" he said concluding with "You will start tomorrow after dinner." Ms Platoron then told Caalin to follow her and she escorted him from the office. "You will meet Professor Grundor in his office right after dinner", she reminded him as he left to go back to his dorm.

He slowly made his way back to the dorm, and the minute he walked through the door everyone bombarded him with questions. They had been waiting for him to return and wanted to know everything that happened with the headmaster. Caalin took a seat and went over all the details from the meeting. He told them what the punishment was, and how he would have to endure a full week with Dargon. Ssam gulped, "What do you think Professor Grundor has planned for the two of you." Caalin looked up, "I don't know, something about geological samples that need to be broken down, and I don't think it is going to be fun."

They all set down to do the required reading that had to be complete for their next day of classes, then eased off to their rooms and bed. The next day seemed so peaceful, even Dargon was not his obnoxious self, so the day went by quickly and quietly. After dinner both Caalin and Dargon made their way to Professor Grundor's office for detention.

Professor Grundor met them just outside his office with two large hammers. He gave one to each of them saying, "Normally we use laser hammers for this, but the headmaster seems to think you will benefit more from a little manual labor." He then led them through his office and out a door in the back. As they went through the door, they entered a large hanger with contained several huge rocks. Professor Grundor pointed to two large rocks next to each other and told the boys, "you are to break up both rocks, then place the smaller pieces in the containers in the corner. You may go, when both of you have completed the task. If one of you finishes before the other you can either wait or help him and leave earlier. It would be entirely up to the two of you, but no one leaves until both of you have completed." He then turn and went back into his office.

Caalin looked a Dargon and asked, "Which rock do you want?" Dargon quickly turned toward the rock nearest him, "I'll take this one" and began to hammer away at it. The boys hammered as hard and as fast as they could and the rocks begin to crumble under each blow of the hammers. Once the rocks had been broken down, they began to fill the containers. After what seemed like forever, but was only about three hours, the boys had the containers filled and went back into the office to inform the Professor. He walked out into the hanger, surveyed the work, "Very good, you may go now." The boys left as fast as they could so not to give the professor a chance to change his mind. As they left the office the boys turned and took off in separate directions toward their dorms neither of them saying a word to the other.

When Caalin reached his dorm, his friends met him the moment he entered the room. Ssophia look at Caalin with a startling look on her face, "Caalin you're bleeding!" Ang quickly grabbed his hands and looked at them, they were bleeding badly. Ang and Ssophia grabbed him by his arms and drug him back through the door, and off to the infirmary to have his hands looked at.

At the infirmary, the nurse looked at his hand, cleaned them, put some sort of medication on them and then bandaged them. She told him, "They will be ok within twenty-four hours." As she was cleaning up the mess she told the girls, "He is the second boy to come in with bleeding blisters this evening." They quickly guessed that Dargon had the same problem as Caalin. After the nurse finished the paperwork on Caalin's injury she released them. They made their way back to the dorm with the girls complaining about the severity of the punishment all the way back, but all Caalin wanted was to get back and go to bed.

The next day at breakfast, sure enough Dargon's had bandages on both of his hands. The day was not going well for Caalin, he had to do more supervising than actual work on the racer during engineering class, and had problems during self-defense, but otherwise the day was fairly quite. That evening when he and Dargon showed up for their detention, Professor Grundor quickly put them to work just sorting rocks instead of breaking them up. The rest of their week of detention went by quietly. They spent it either sorting rocks or labeling containers and did not have to break down any more large rocks. Their hands healed by the second day as the nurse had told them and by the end of the week. Everything was back to normal, and Caalin was happy to be able to work on the skyracer again.

Every evening while Caalin was doing his detention, Mouse and Ssam would go over the racer plans and look at other designs on the computer. They had come up with the idea of mounting two engines that extended out on both sides of the cockpit; this would make the racer handle better. They also wanted to put larger wings closer to the front to make the racer more stable during flight. They discussed this with Caalin, and he thought it was a great idea.

Finally, the day came and the racer was complete. It now had two small crystal impulse engines, extended out from the rear cockpit on both sides and the wings were placed more to the front to make the handling better. They had painted it dark red and placed the Bangalors logo on both sides. The Beta's racer was looking almost complete also; it looked like a reverse drop of water with two small engines mounted right next to the Cockpit underneath the wings. It was a shiny silver color with the Beta logo on both sides.

Finishing the racer was great because the freshman race was in two weeks, and to the winners goes a large trophy that is placed in the trophy case in the main common area. The trophy will have the names of all the winning squad members on it for public display. In addition to the trophy 10,000 points awarded toward the Squadron of Excellence Award, which at the end of the year goes to the squad with the most points for the combine effort of all members of the freshman squads. The rest of the points divided with second place getting 6,000, third getting 3,000 and last place gets 1,500.

CHAPTER 8

ssam's secret

It was now a week before the race, Mouse awoke in the middle of the night; he had a dream that someone was tampering with their racer. He quickly woke up Caalin and Ssam and told them what was bothering him. Ssam told him, "go back to sleep it was only a dream everything was ok." But Mouse could not sleep and finally talked the other two into going with him to check on the racer. They got out of their beds and slowly got dress. Quietly they made their way from their room, across their common area, out the door and into the hallway. They walked slowly through the halls toward the engineering classroom trying not to make any noise.

As they neared the engineering classroom, Ssam stepped back and said, "Someone is coming our way." He grabbed both Caalin's and Mouse's arms and pushed them back against the wall as he did Dargon and his two cohorts, Jon and Devolon came walking around the corner. They walked right pass them as if they were not there. Dargon was Laughing and said to the other two, "they'll be surprised come race day." Mouse looked over to Ssam but could not see him. He could feel Ssam's hand gripping his arm but Ssam was not there, this cause Mouse to let out a little yelp. Dargon stopped and looked back down the hall to see where the sound had come from but saw nothing that could have made the noise. He turned to Jon and Devolon. "We needed to hurry someone must be coming." They ran down the hall, being as quite as they could, trying to get back to their dorm before someone saw them.

Mouse was still staring at were Ssam should be and all of a sudden Ssam and Caalin reappeared. Mouse was looking at Ssam with a bewildered expression on his face. Ssam seeing his expression calmly said, "Oh, I never mentioned that Ssophia and I have the ability to bend light around ourselves and whatever we are touching? It allows us to blend into the surrounding background and makes us almost completely invisible, but you almost gave us away." "Sorry but I thought I was seeing things or not seeing things I should say", Mouse replied. "How did you do that?" asked Caalin. Ssam said, "I will explain it later when we get back to our room." Mouse quickly reminded them that Dargon had come out of the engineering classroom and that they needed to see what they were up to in there.

The boys entered the classroom and went straight to their racer. They could not see anything externally wrong with the racer itself, so they went over to look at the beta racer, it look fine also. They decided they would get with the other squads during breakfast and tell them what happened. Leaving the classroom they made their way down the hall, back across the common area, and down their hallway toward the dorm room. Tomorrow they would have to do a complete check on their system to make sure everything was fine and working properly. There was no telling what the Delta's did and to be safe they would have to run the tests.

Ssam looked over at Caalin and Mouse and told them that he would like it if they would not tell anyone about how they avoided the Delta's in the hallway. Mouse and Caalin quickly let him know that it would be their secret and no one else would know, but he would have to explain how he did it. Ssam reminded them he had said he would when they got back to their room.

Soon they were lying in bed and Ssam was telling them about his grandparents on his father's side of the family. He told them how the two of had met. They were both scientist working on an Alliance project to build a stealth fighter during the pirate war. The Fighter was supposed to be able to bend light around it to make it completely invisible to any detection. They both worked on different parts of the systems and were somehow exposed to a lot of different types of radiation. During their time working on the project they fell in love and got married, but when Ssam's grandmother became pregnant she left the project and returned home. She lived with my great grandparents until my father was born. My grandfather was able to be home on leave with her for a short period of time after the birth, but he had to go back after three weeks and that was the last my grandmother saw of him. The pirates raided the planet where they were working on the fighter, destroying all the hangers and everyone in them, my grandfather's body and one of another scientist were never recovered.

He also told them about his mother's father who had been working on another project for the Alliance to create a material to make uniforms that could change color and blend in with the background. He was a chemist and was injured in a chemical explosion in his lab.

Ssophia and I are the only people from our planet that have the ability bend light. Doctors think the exposure to the radiation must have affected our father's parents DNA and the chemicals that our mother's father was exposed to could have altered his DNA as well. That change morphed over a period and was passed down and when we were born. It seems the combination changed our DNA to give us the ability to bend light and blend into our surroundings. They think the change happened in our parents and they passed it to use. This is also the very thing that got us both sent here; we would use our abilities to slip into theatrical performances we were restricted from seeing. Ok now you know how we are able to bend light and why we are here, I am tired so let's go to sleep.

The boys had just went back to sleep when the girls started banging on their door shouting for them to get up or they would miss breakfast. They slowly got out of bed still dressed from their little excursion and made their way out to meet the girls.

The minute they reached the dining hall, Mouse and Ssam went over to the Beta table while Caalin stopped by the Charlie table and asked them to join him and the others. Once everyone were together Caalin told them what they saw and heard in the hallway and suggested everyone check their racers to make sure Dargon and the Delta goons had not tampered with them. Jason Rogers from Charlie squad asked, "Are you sure they tampered with our racers?" Caalin replied, "We are not sure, but from what we heard it is possible, so to be on the safe side we need to check." "We want the race to be a fair race and I don't want the Delta squadron wining it." Everyone agreed and decided to go over their racers and check everything.

CHAPTER 9

The Practice Run

The next week Alpha, Beta and Charlie squads spent time checking and double-checking their racers. They had to make sure that there was nothing missed and everything was perfect. Three days before the race, each squadron had practice runs scheduled and it was now time to select the pilots for the racers. The Alpha team quickly decided that Caalin would be their pilot because he had flown a racer before. Beta team's pilot was Clair Tilone a small cute girl with greenish blue hair. Charlie Squadron was Jason Rogers; all the girls thought he was handsome with his long blond hair and broad shoulders. Finally, the Delta group's pilot was Dargon but everyone knew he would be since he seemed to be their leader anyway. Each squadron had a different time to test their racers so they would not all be on the practice course at the same time. Alpha practice time would be the first two hours after breakfast.

It was the morning of the practice run so the boys got dressed quickly, skipped breakfast and went straight to engineering to get the racer ready. On the way to breakfast Ang asked Ssophia "do you think we should take the boys something to eat?' Ssophia came back with" If we don't they will be complaining later about being hungry." They brought the boys some food and received a loud thank you from Mouse and Ssam as they quickly started eating. When Ang handed Caalin his, he smiled, "Thanks for going out of your way to make sure we didn't go hungry." Ang turned a bright red and said it wasn't that big of a deal. After finishing the food they connected the racer to the electric dolly they had borrowed from the schools maintenance department, then pulled it out of the engineering bay and down to the practice course. Caalin was suited up and carrying his helmet under is right arm. Ssophia was the only one of the group that seems to be able to stay calm under pressure so she would maintain communications between the pit crew and Caalin. Once on the starting pad, Caalin put on his helmet, climbed into the racer and began to run through the safety checks on the system and the controls. Mouse would read them off to Ssophia who would relay them to Caalin over the radio. After about ten minutes of checks and double checks, they had the go ahead from Professor Marru and Professor Taran. Professor Taran was there because he was the Alpha squad advisor and wanted to see how his freshmen's racer would perform, and Professor Marru was in charge of the practice runs.

Caalin started the engines and it purred like a Salvian Mirse cat, he hit the lifter thrusters and the racer began to rise above the pad. He then began to throttle up and the ship slowly began to move forward. Ssophia told Caalin, "Take the first run slow and easy to get a feel of how the racer handled and get familiar with the course, then you can increase your speed on the second run." Each group only gets three runs, so the third run Caalin would want to give it all he could.

Caalin took it out slowly on the first run and the racer was handling great as he studied the course. After he made the first lap, he increased his speed by two thirds. Then when he came around for the third run he opened the racer full throttle giving it all he could and zoomed pass the grand stand where everyone was watching. After the last run, he brought the racer to a safe and easy landing.

Ssam and Mouse ran down to meet him as he began to run through all the shut down procedures and final checks. Everything was good to go and the group quickly towed their ship back up the hill and into the engineering bay. Once back in the bay they grabbed all their test equipment and started running tests on every part of the racer. By the time, they had finished testing and recalibrating things it was time for lunch.

The Beta squadron had made their practice run while Alpha was doing their tests on their systems. The Beta crew had just returned to the engineering bay with their ship and secured it, they would come back after lunch to run all their final tests. Joining the Alpha squad they all headed toward the dining hall for lunch.

During lunch, Charlie squad came by to find out how the test runs went and what the test course was like. Beta was bragging about how well their racer handled during the practice runs and how well Clair had piloted it. After lunch everyone had free time, Alpha went straight to the dorm room, and Beta returned to the engineering bay to run their test on their racer. Charlie was now out on the practice course, and no one cared where Delta squad was.

However, the Delta boys had found a location in one of the schools towers where they could see the practice course and watch everyone's performances. They made notes on every practice run made by the other squads. They hoped this would give them the opportunity to make changes to their racer to give them a little more advantage over the others. Moreover, Dargon could see how the pilots handled their racers.

After dinner that evening Alpha, Beta and Charlie squads met back in the dining hall to play some board games, relax and talk about their practice runs that day. The excitement was high about the upcoming race and everyone was having a good time until the Delta squad arrived

Dargon made a loud comment, "delta's racer was the best and no one will be able to top him in the race." Mouse popped up and said, "Caalin would leave him in his ion vapor trail." Dargon laughed, "You're full of yourself; no Alliance lizard could beat him." Caalin made a move toward Dargon when Ssophia and Ang both grabbed him by the arms. Dargon laughed again and said, "Your girls are right to hold you back, you might get hurt this time Matthews." Then he and the Deltas got up and made their way back out the door. Caalin was angry with the girls and asked them why they stopped him. Ang said, "You do want to fly in the race don't you?" "If you had started something it would have gotten you detention again plus grounded from flying," Ssophia added. Then a voice came from the back of the dining hall, "the girls are right, you would have been grounded" It was Headmaster Keayan. "I watch all the practice runs today; you all have good ships and fine pilots. I'm looking forward to the race, so don't do anything to spoil it for me." After that statement the headmaster walked out of the dining hall and off toward his office. It was getting late so everyone said good night and made their way back to their dorms.

CHAPTER 10

The skyracer Race

The next day everything was back to normal everyone was back in class and the day was going by without any problems. They all used engineering class time to work on their racers and make last minute adjustments. The only thing they got from Delta squad that day was just sneers and angry looks. Someone said the headmaster had a little talk with the group about the night before.

Every meal that day was filled with excitement and talk about the big race. That evening everyone found it difficult to sleep with thoughts of the race in their heads. The next morning it was hard to eat breakfast because everyone was nervous and excited about the race. After breakfast, they made their way to the engineering bay and began preparing their racers.

The Alpha squad was hard at work, Ssophia checked out the communication systems, Ssam and Mouse checked all the fuel lines and wiring, while Ang and Caalin went down the preflight checklist. Everything checked out perfect so they towed the ship down to the starting line. At the starting line, they finally got a good look at the Charlie racer; it looked like an egg with two small engines the extended out three feet on both sides. The Delta racer however look like a small sword, with a cone shape cockpit and to wings that curve forward on both sides and it was the only racer in the race with just one engine.

The grand stands were setup on both sides of the final portion of the course all the way to the finish line. There were large monitors placed throughout the stands that were linked to cameras all along the race route. This would give everyone a good view of the entire course so they would not miss any of the race. Headmaster Keayan's voice came over the intercom, "The race was about to begin, all pilots know the route and the rules, anyone not following the rules precisely will be disqualified." He continued," Pilots prepare your ships for takeoff." Caalin put on his helmet and made another communications check with Ssophia. Then climbed into the racer and began the pre-launch checklist. Ssophia, Ang, Ssam and Mouse move into the lower portion of the stands designated for the pit crews and monitors would allowed them to see everything going on in the race and the cockpit of their racer.

"Racers power up your engines" came over the communications system. Caalin fire up the engine and slowly started to hover above the starting pad. Once every ship was hovering above their pads, the voice came over the communications system again, "all systems ready, on your mark and go!"

The ships blasted from the pads, and pass the stands filled with their cheering upper classmates. Fifty kilometers out, they made a sharp turn to the right through a narrow canyon path that was marked with sensors. Racing through the canyons, the lead kept swapping from one racer to another. One minute Beta would be in the lead, the next Delta, then Charlie and Alpha.

They ran down through valleys and dark caverns that went through the mountains. Once through the caverns and out into a clearing they made another right turn. Finally, they came out into the home stretch across a long flat plain toward the stands. This was lap one of three laps they had to make in the race. On second lap Dargon bumped the Beta racer a couple of times as he passed Clair on her right side. They were now made their way down the stretch through the stands again when Dargon bumped Jason in the Charlie squad's racer.

It was now the last lap and Dargon was challenging Caalin for the lead. They swapped the lead several time as they went through the valleys and caverns. Now everyone was on the final stretch and headed for the finish line. Suddenly the Beta ship started to lose power and slowed almost to a crawl, and then Charlie's racer started losing its power and slowing down. It then became a one on one race between Delta and Alpha. Caalin gave it all he could and passed Dargon in the Delta racer. As he passed, Dargon maneuvered his racer to give Caalin hard bump. This knock Caalin's ship a little off course but he was able to keep it in the designated race area so as not to be disqualified.

Caalin pushed the ship hard giving it full throttle, when suddenly his right engine burst into flames and smoke begin to pour out the exhaust vents. He had the lead by a few meters and was determined to keep it. As they neared the finish line Dargon was getting closer and was trying to pass, it was neck and neck. Then just as they crossed the finish line, left engine exploded into flames, on Caalin's racer.

Thinking fast Caalin immediately pulled up with his racer steering it away from the stands and the other students. Once he had cleared the stands and pointed the racer toward an open area so no one could get hurt, then he ejected from the cockpit. The canopy blew off the cockpit and his seat flew out.

The canopy was suddenly caught by a gust of wind, blew back at Caalin hitting him in flight. He was hit with such force that it fractured his left arm and knocked him unconscious. The parachute on the ejection seat deployed automatically and slowly began lowering him toward the ground. There was another large gust of wind and Caalin's chute drifted into a tree snagging at the top. There he was unconscious and hanging helplessly from the tree still strapped in the seat which was now upside down.

Students and faculty began filing from the stands and running toward the crash site. Ang saw Caalin hanging in the tree and not moving. She quickly spread her wings and took flight, flying as fast as she could toward Caalin passing everyone on the ground. This seemed like the fastest she had ever flown in her life. When she reached Caalin, she called his name but no movement. She quickly removed his helmet and dropped it to the ground, then checked his pulse. She was relieved; he still had a heartbeat and was breathing. She slowly disconnected his straps of his harness while hanging on to him tightly. Then slowly she flew him down to the ground and the now waiting crowed below.

Headmaster Keayan, Professor Marru, and Professor Taran were there by the time Ang had him on the ground and told all the students to stand back. Mouse, Ssam and Ssophia came bursting through the crowed just as the emergency vehicles arrived. They loaded Caalin on a stretcher and put him in the ambulance and Ang quickly jumped in after him. Professor Marru tried to stop her but the Headmaster told him to let her go. She turned and yelled to the others to take care what was left of the racer, that they would need to find out what cause the fires.

Mouse and Ssam quickly ran back to the pit area to get the dolly they use to move the ship as Ssophia went straight to the crash site. When she got there the fire crew had just finished extinguishing the flaming wreckage. Once they all were at the site they begin to pick up the pieces and load them on the dolly. Everyone from Beta and Charlie squads quickly came to help them and after about thirty minutes, they had everything on the dolly and hauled it back to the hanger bay. Charlie and Beta Squad pulled their ships in a few minutes later. Ssam look around and saw the Delta Squad's ship was already there but they were nowhere in sight.

Once they had secured the ship, what was left of it, Ssophia, Mouse and Ssam ran out of the bay and down the hallways toward the medical wing. When they reached the Medical bay, Ang was there to meet them. As they entered she quickly told them, "Caalin is ok, he came to in the ambulance and I let him know he won. Once they got him to the Medical wing, they examined him. They said he has a concussion and a broken arm, but he will be fine. They have him in the regeneration chamber and should be back to his old self in a couple of days."

Ssam asked, "What's regeneration chamber?" Mouse popped in telling him, "It is a vacuum-sealed chamber filled with pure oxygen. They place you in and then injected you with nanobots that repair you body on the molecular level. This allows a person to heal in two or three days instead of weeks or months." Ssam seemed relieved to hear this and then joked that Caalin would do anything to miss a few days of classes. This gave the four of them a good and needed laugh.

Mouse and Ssam left and went back to the hanger bay to start going through the parts of what was left of the racer. Ang and Sophia stayed behind just in case there were any more updates on Caalin's condition. The boys wanted to reassemble the racer in hopes to find out what went wrong before Caalin got out of the medical wing.

The Beta and Charlie groups had just walked in to look over their racers and saw the two Alpha squad members there. Everyone went over to find out how Caalin was doing. Ssam was happy to tell them everything Ang had told him. The two groups decided to help them with their inspection of the racer. Piece by piece they went over every part of the ship not destroyed by the flames. They all worked late into the night, but could not find anything to tell them what went wrong. Later back at the dorm room the boys let the girls in on what they had been doing and the girls updated them on Caalin's condition.

The next day was a day off from classes, so Ssam and Mouse decided after breakfast they would go back to the hanger bay and go over the ship one more time. The girls would go to the medical wing and check on Caalin's progress. When the boys got to the hanger the Beta squad was there going over their ship and the Charlie group came in right behind Mouse and Ssam. Clair Tilone the Beta pilot came over to talk to Ssam. She had a small electronic device about the size of button in her hand. She told him, "We found this planted on our plasma drive computer. It was giving of and electrical pulse that interrupted the plasma flow just enough to slow our ship down." This was why Beta came in last place; it had crippled their engines enough that they crawled across the finish line just behind Charlie Squadron.

Just then Jason Rogers from Charlie came over with had a similar device in his hand, that had done the same thing to their racer. Ssam and Mouse quickly started looking over their ship for a similar device. Both Beta and Charlie groups came over and joined in again to help.

After what seemed like hours, they found a device similar but a little larger. Gahe Gluskap, one of the Charlie boys, said that it was something you would put on a plasma line to cause it to leak and a leaking plasma line can cause a fire in an engine compartment. That is what Dargon had done to their racer the night they caught the Delta boys coming out of the engineering bay. Mouse said, "We need to tell the girls and Caalin about this."

They quickly thanked the others and told them they would see them at lunch. The two ran out of the bay and down the hallway toward the medical wing. Once they entered the medical wing, they were happy to see Caalin setting up talking with the girls. They ran over and both of them, at the same time, tried to tell them what they had found. Ssophia said, "Wait a minute you two, one of you at a time." They looked at each other and then both tried to tell them again, both at the same time. Ssophia stopped them again, she then look at Ssam, "What in the world are you two talking about?" Ssam told them what Beta and Charlie found on their racers and that they all pitched in to help look though the Alpha racer and found this. He then held up the small half melted device so Caalin could see it. Mouse quickly chimed in with the fact that it was something you would put on a plasma line that would cause it to leak and a leaking plasma line could have been what caused the engine fire. Caalin look around at everyone and then told them all, "there is nothing we can do about it." Ang looked at him surprised, "We need to go to the Headmaster about it." "And tell him what?" replied Caalin. "That Delta squad sabotaged our ships," said Ang. "What proof do we have that they did it?" asked Caalin. "We can tell him what we over heard them saying in the hallway the night we caught them coming out of engineering!" chimed Mouse. Ssam looked at him, "Then how are we going to explain what we were doing that night, he may think we sabotaged the other ships!" "Oh, I didn't think about that" Mouse said. Ssophia was shocked "You over heard them saying they did something to our ship and didn't tell us?" "We told the Beta and Charlie boys we heard them talking about something, and went over our racer with a fine tooth comb, but we didn't find anything, not even this." said Caalin. He pickup the small piece of metal "we must have just over looked it; it does look a lot like a coupling." Ssophia and Ang look at each other then at the very same time said "BOYS!" they then got up, with angry looks on their faces left the room and went back toward the dorm.

Just as the girls were leaving the room, the nurse came walking in. She turned to watch the girls leave and then looked over to the boys, "you boys really made them mad didn't you?" The boys just looked at each other and laughed. Then nurse then told Caalin, "Mr. Matthews since you are doing so well the doctor is releasing you to go back to classes." She also told him, "You cannot do any heavy lifting for five days and will have to come back in for a checkup. We will send you a reminder to let him know when." Caalin jumped from his bed and began getting dressed. They would just have enough time to get to the dining hall for lunch and with any luck beat the crowds.

At lunch, everyone was surprised and happy to see Caalin up and about. Ang and Ssophia were so surprised they forgot they were mad at the boys. Everybody came by and asked him how he was and had he heard anything about the investigation. Caalin look at Ang and then asked, "What investigation, did you two go to the headmaster?" Ang shook her head no and told him that Professor Taran told them about it just before they came in for lunch. "It is mandatory they investigate because a student was injured," said Clair. She continued "Everyone has to turn over anything found that was not original to their racers to the squadron advisors. Jason told me he heard that Delta turned in a device similar to the one we found. They told Professor Ravin they found it on their ship attached to the plasma line, but it must have not gone off." Ssam gritted his teeth, "Yeah I bet they found it on their ship, more like in their pockets." Mouse just nodded his head in agreement with Ssam. "Well there is no way to prove it was the Delta Group", said Caalin. "But we can keep our eye on them," snapped Ssam.

---- C H A P T E R   1 1 ----

End of the first semester

The next couple of weeks were more of the same with all they classes and the end of the semester was coming up. Caalin had been back to the medical wing and the doctor had given him a clean bill of health. The investigation of the crash went nowhere and no one got the blame for the sabotage. The end of semester banquet would be in two weeks along with the awarding of the trophy and points for the race. The trophies went in the Squadron awards cabinet in the main common area and each member of the teams receives a medal for their uniform.

Classes were going great, Delta group were their usual obnoxious selves, but all and all everything was fine. Everyone seems to wonder what the next semester class schedule would look like; they should be getting their schedule and books soon. That evening when they returned to the dorms, they found books and a new schedule setting on the table in the common room. They picked up the schedule and went over it.

Alpha Squad class schedules for 2nd Semester
0700 - 0830 Universal History - Professor Taran
0830 - 0945 Engineering –Professor Marru
0945- 1100 Self Defense - Professor Kai
1100-1200 Lunch
1200 -1315 Politics and Diplomacy –Professor EaHaci

1315 -1430 Universal Botany - Professor Ravin
1430 -1545 Universal Geology - Professor Grundor
1545 -1645 Dinner
1645 -1800 Universal languages –Professor Qua Chai

Some of the classes had been shifted around; Alpha now had Self-defense with Delta, a new class Politics and Diplomacy with Beta and Universal Geology with Charlie. Then there was an extra class at the end of the day Universal languages with all the groups together, plus it would be after dinner.

The girls were worried about the extra class, but the boys were looking forward to the self-defense class with Delta squad. It would be a lot of fun throwing them around the classroom and getting a little revenge on Dargon and his goons.

Finally, the day of the end of semester banquet was here. The boys were looking forward to the awards ceremony and the girls were looking forward to seeing all the boys in their dress uniforms. They spent most of the day polishing their boots and preparing their uniforms for the evening. That evening the boys got dressed and met the girls in the common room. The girls immediately started correcting problems with the boy's uniforms. Ang was straightening Caalin's collar, "You look good in your dress uniform, too bad you can't wear it more often." Caalin looked at her a little confused and she just smiled and turned to help Mouse.

They met with the rest of the squads in the large common area and they all entered the dining hall as a group making their way to their seats. Ra was at the head of their table since he was the student deputy advisor for Alpha squadron. After about ten minutes of confusion all the squadrons were in the dining hall and seated.

Ra stood up walked over to the door next to the instructor tables opened it and yelled, "All Rise". The entire student body stood as the headmaster and the staff filed into the dining hall. They made their way pass a large table that held a huge trophy and lots of awards until they reached their seats and stood behind their chairs. Once everyone was in place they took their seats and Ra yelled "Be seated" and the students took their seats.

Professor Kai stood up, cleared her throat and said, "I would like to make a short announcement for the first year students. We have obtained permission from everyone's parents or guardians for all of you to take the yearly school trip. Therefore on the third week of the second semester everyone will be going to Parinta` for a day." Parinta` is a small city on Maratalo the closes planet to the cat's eye nebula in which the academy is located. She continued, "Professors EaHaci, Qua Chai and I will be the school escorts and we will be holding squadron deputy advisors responsible for each of their squadrons while in Parinta`." She then took her seat and the Headmaster stood up, "It is time for the awards and honors to be given out, but first I would like to announce the appointment of the new assistant deputy advisors for each squadron." He then went down a list of upper classmen from each squadron.

Each person he called off from the upper classes would become the squadron deputy advisors at the end of the second semester. Each one would be training with the current deputy advisors until assuming the position themselves. At the end of the semester, the current deputy advisors will become a staff assistant. Squadron deputy advisors become staff assistant their last year at the school. This allows them the opportunity to learn how to manage a large command and what goes on in day-to-day operations.

The headmaster then moved on down his list of awards and honors until he finally got to the freshman class. This is what Caalin, Mouse, and Ssam had been waiting for. "To remind everyone that this year's freshman race was marred with an accident, that thank goodness was not a fatal one," he said. He then looked down at Caalin "However thanks to the piloting abilities and courage of young Mister Matthews he was able to maneuver his ship away from the stands to avoid a major disaster." He paused for a second then continued "With this said we award Caalin Matthews with a special medal of courage for his heroic act of bravery."

Caalin rose and walked up to the podium and the headmaster placed the medal around his neck. He began to turn to walk back to his seat when the headmaster told him to wait. Then he said, "Although he crashed his racer Mister Matthews did manage to finish in first place and with that I would like to call up the rest of his squad to except their awards, Angiliana Avora, Mortomous Valtor, Ssamuel and Ssophia Ssallazz." The headmaster paused again then said, "I would also like to present an award of commendation to Ms. Avora for her speed, courage and ability to assist in the rescue of Mister Matthews after the crash, if not for her assistance no telling how long it would have taken to retrieve Mister Matthews from the tree he was dangling from." The Delta squad snickered at this comment, and the Beta and Charlie groups gave them angry looks. He then awarded them the first place trophy and placed the medals around their necks. They took the trophy back though the cheering upper classes and their friends in Beta and Charlie Squads, returning to their seats at the Alpha table. The headmaster continued giving out the rest of the awards. Caalin cringed when he awarded the Delta squadron with second place but cheered loudly for the Beta and Charlie groups when they received their awards.

After all the awards had been handed out the headmaster looked out at everyone, he then held out his arms and said. "Let the banquet begin". With that said the food started coming out from all doors of the kitchen. Everyone was hungry and there was everything you could imagine food wise. There were breads, meats, vegetables and most of all the deserts and the boys did their best to eat their share of it.

After the banquet, the boys complained that they had eaten too much while making their way back to the dorms, and The girls did not show them any sympathy for doing it either. Once they reached the dorm they all went straight to their rooms, changed out of their dress uniforms and went straight to bed.

CHAPTER 12

second semester begins

The next day was the first day of the new semester, most of the classes they had the first semester went the same, the only exception was self-defense, which did not go as well as Mouse and Ssam had hoped. The two of them hoped to be tossing the Delta boys across the room but instead spent a lot of their time flying through the air as well. Caalin faired a lot better in the class and Dargon did his best to avoid having to face off against him.

In Engineering they were working on rebuilding the skyracer and improving its performance. They had went through every part of it and made changes to almost every component on the racer,

Universal Languages had Professor Qua Chai giving them a list of twenty words to learn. He then told them they would get a new list daily to learn and would be tested on them two days before their trip to Parinta`. These were words they would have to use in conversation while there and he would have their upper classmates monitoring them to see how well they used the words while communicating with the locals.

In Politics and Diplomacy Professor EaHaci gave them a stack of political reviews to read that analyzed polices put into place by the Planetary Alliance. This required a lot of reading that night and Caalin found himself having difficulty pronouncing a lot of the words they were assigned. Ang asked Caalin "would like some help with the language assignment." He let out a quick, "Yes!" They spent most of the evening setting at the far end of the table in the common area going over the words and their meanings. Caalin would mispronounce a word and Ang would giggle then tell him the correct pronunciation and the meaning. He asked Ang. "how do you know so much about the language we're trying to learn?" She told him, "My home planet does a lot of trade with Maratalo and I have many friends from there." Caalin look up at Mouse and he was at the other end of the table helping both Ssam and Ssophia. Then Ang reach across the table, patted Caalin's hand, and told him,"We needed to get back to the words." He looked over to her smiled and then went back to attempting to pronounce another word.

Every day they would get new words and every night Ang would help Caalin and Mouse would help Ssam and Ssophia. Finally, it was test day Caalin was so nervous he thought he would forget everything Ang had helped him with. As they were entering the classroom, Ang grabbed his hand and he turned to face her. She looked straight into his eyes, "you're going to do great on the test you know all the words and their meanings." He smiled at the thought that she had that much confidence in him.

The test was a hard one, there were words on it that looked similar to the words they had studied, but some of the letters were in different places in the word. There were definitions of words that were close to what some of the words meant, but were not the correct meaning. Caalin scratched his head and sweat ran down his face throughout the entire test. After the test was over Professor Qua Chai told them, they could leave for the rest of the period and they would get the results the next day.

Back in the dorm, they all set around discussing the test and what they thought were the correct answers. Ssam would mention a word on the test and the definition he thought he put down and Mouse would tell him that it was wrong. Caalin just set there listening knowing he had totally failed the test. Ang saw the worried look on Caalin's face, "Don't worry you did great, just look at who tutored you", they both broke into laughter. Ssophia was just setting there enjoying Mouse tormenting Ssam, knowing that most of the answers Mouse told him were wrong were indeed correct.

The next day in engineering class the group was putting the finish tough on their racer. They had spent most of their engineering class time over the past few weeks rebuilding it with the help of the Beta group.

Finally, it was all back together and looking better than it did before. The Beta group had repaired their ship and to keep busy had decided to help the Alpha group.

They were now learning about the workings of dimensional jump systems. During their down time in class, Caalin and Mouse would pour over books and diagrams on the different types of jump systems. This was something that really caught their curiosity and they wanted to learn as much about it as possible. Mouse downloaded some manuals and diagrams from the engineering computer so they could study them in the dorm.

Even self-defense class got better as Caalin finally got a chance to face off with Dargon. Whenever he had the chance he threw him as hard and as far as he could across the room. He threw him so hard one time that Professor Kai had to reprimand him, but she did it with a small smile on her face.

After class they met with Charlie and Beta groups for lunch and Ssam would go over how many times Caalin tossed Dargon across the room and the look on Dargon's face every time he got up off the floor. Everyone laughed; even Ang and Ssophia found it amusing the way Ssam told it. The Delta squad just set at their table and sneered in their direction. Dargon whispered to the Delta squad in a low voice that the Alphas would get theirs and soon.

CHAPTER 13

Trip to Parinta

The day for the trip to Parinta` had finally arrived. The ships were in the docking bay and everyone was in their dorms getting prepared. When they reached the docking bay there were three ships, each of the professors had one of the ships assigned to them. Students could board whatever ship they wanted but had to check in with the professor in charge of the ship as they boarded. While Caalin and the rest of Alpha squad were deciding which ship to board the Beta and Charlie groups came wondering up. Everyone wanted to know which ship they wanted to board. Together they all decided to board Professor Kai's ship.

As they were boarding they notice that all the Delta students both upper and lower classmen were all getting on the same ship, the one with Professor EaHaci. The other two ships were a mixture of the other three squadrons. "Deltas don't mix with other groups very often," said one of the Beta upper classmates as he walked pass.

Everyone board boarded the shuttle, checked in with Professor Kai, and took a seat. After all were aboard and seated Professor Kai checked in with the other instructors. They synchronized their computers to verify that they had everyone. Synchronizing their computers gave them all a list of everyone on all three ships. She then went to the front of the ship and took her seat. She picked up the microphone and told the pilot everything was a go for takeoff.

The shuttle doors closed and the ships slowly lifted off the ground and moved away from the docking bay. Moments later were exiting the planet's atmosphere and cruising through the nebula. Once they were clear of the nebula there was a flash and a jerk, it was the dimensional jump engines. Professor Kai came over the intercom and told everyone "We will be landing in about thirty minutes." The window shielding lifted and now everyone could see the planet coming up in front of the ship. The planet was a mixture of blue, green, brown and white.

The white was the polar caps on the north and south ends of the planet. As they moved closer, they could see the forest thick with trees and brush. There were fields of planted crops and snow capped mountains scattered here and there. They soon entered the atmosphere and cruised slowly over the beautiful green fields. The ships landed at a docking station just outside of the city.

Professor Kai announced, "For those of you that have never visited Parinta` before please wait for me in the docking bay. You will then follow me to the control center and afterwards I will show you to the land shuttle area. For those of you that have visited before, there is no reason to wait, you are free to continue on your own." Once she had completed her announcement the ship touched down and the doors slowly began to open.

Students from the upper classes hurried to get off and get through the control center not wanting to waste any precious time. The freshman classes remain together and follow Professor Kai to the control center. Everyone landing on Maratalo has to go through the control center for decontamination procedures. The planet provides a lot of fruit, vegetables and other plants to thousands of other planets and any bugs or viruses that may come in on visitors could cause serious damage to the crops.

Once through the Control Center they came to a smaller docking area for land shuttles. Once there Professor Kai told everyone, "this is where I leave you on your own; you will need to be back here by eighteen hundred hours for the return trip to the school." She then continued, "I hope you all have a good, but safe time. If anyone gets into any trouble please look for an upper classmate, they will be more than happy to help you."

The group climbed into the shuttle that had just pulled in to the bay; once everyone took their seat, the shuttle took off toward the city. As they came into the city Caalin could see tall circular buildings, small domes shaped buildings and square shaped buildings. There were buildings with shops in them and open-air markets, Parinta` had a little of everything. The group consisting of the entire Alpha, Beta and Charlie freshmen banded together to see as much of the city as they could before they had to be back to the dock to meet the professor.

Everyone got off the land shuttle at the far end of the city and then begin working their way from there. They went in to candy shops that had exotic flavors of candy, pet stores with strange looking animals and souvenir shops that had things that some of them had never seen before. In one of the pet shops Ssam found a Bangalor Dragon that looked exactly like the one on their logo patch, but the students were not allowed pets so he had to past on buying it. He had gotten a little too close to it and the dragon almost set his shirt on fire, at the amusement of the rest of the group.

After what seemed like hours of wandering, everyone decided to stop at an open-air café for lunch. They pull every free table available together to make room for everyone to set together. They ordered saron sodas, bakara shakes and delphar tea for drinks. They ordered all kinds of things on the menu to eat and when the food arrived, everyone shared it with each other like a small buffet. This allowed them all to sample a variety of the foods found on the planet.

While everyone was still eating Mouse decided he wanted to look in a store next door that had all kinds of gizmos and gadgets in the window. He told everyone what he was going to do as he got up from the table. He then grabbed his drink and wandered over to the store. In the store, he moved from one isle to the next looking up and down the shelves at all the items on them. He was looking at some items on a top shelf as he rounded a corner and ran head-on into Dargon spilling his bakara shake all over him. Dargon immediately became furious and yelled to the Delta boys that were with him, "Grab the little rat! I'll teach him to watch where he's going."

Mouse in fear for his life turned quickly and darted for the door. Devlon made a leap to grab him, but Mouse let out a yelp and darted under a shelf. The Deltas boys were trying to grab him were knocking over shelves and displays. Items were crashing and breaking all over the store as they made their way toward the door.

The noise coming from the store next door got everyone's attention at the café. Mouse came running out of the door followed by two large Deltas in hot pursuit. As he ran pass the restaurant Caalin told Ssam to take care of the bill and tossed him some currency. With one leap Caalin left his chair flew over the table, landed in the street right behind Mouse, and quickly followed him. He ran up alongside of Mouse and told him to turn down a small alley, which they soon found to be a dead end.

They could hear the Deltas catching up; Caalin quickly grabbed Mouse and made a giant leap with him under his arm. Caalin leaped and hit one wall on the left side of the alley then bounced back across to the one on the right and finally to the top of the building on the left. Once they were on the top of the building Caalin let Mouse go.

Mouse scrambled to his feet and looked at Caalin with his eye wide open. "How in the world were you able to do that," he asked. Caalin told him, "I've always been able to lift thing and jump like that, but I will explained it to you later." They then looked back down in to the alley as the Delta boys rounded the corner and entered it. The Deltas scrambled around looking through everything in the alley trying to find them, Caalin covering his mouth so not to laugh. He pulled Mouse away from the edge. They walked over to the other side of the building to see if there was a way down.

Looking down they could see the rest of their friends running toward the alley. Caalin grabbed a piece of wood lying on the top of the building and dropped it right in front of Jason Rogers. He stopped quickly and looked up to see Caalin and Mouse waving at them. The group stopped dead in their tracks. Ssam started to yell up to them when Caalin put his finger to his lips and motioned to stop him. Ang quickly flew up to where they were and asked the question Ssam was about to yell. "How did you get up here we saw you run into the alley?" Caalin told her he would explain later but fist they needed to get off the building. "Can you fly Mouse down?" he asked Ang. She said she could, then lifted Mouse and flew back down to the ground. She turned to go back for Caalin when everyone gasped as he leap from the top of the build bouncing off the side of the building on the other side and then to the ground. He ran over to the group and said, "Let's move on down the street before they come out of the alley." They quickly move down the street in the other direction and into another large shop.

Once in the shop everyone gathered around as Ang asked Caalin again, "how were you able to do that and how did you and Mouse get on top of the building so quickly?" He then told them about the planet he was born on, about how heavy the gravity was and how he was able to do these things because the gravity was far less on this planet. He then looked at Mouse and asked, "Why were they chasing you?" Mouse told them what had happened in the store and everyone got a good laugh visualizing Dargon with bakara shake all over him. Then a voice from behind them said, "Laugh all you want to you little rodent, but I will get you sooner or later." it was Dargon and his crew. "Your friends can't protect you forever, rodent" he said with a sneer and then turned as he and the Deltas left the shop. Caalin told Mouse, "stay close and do not wonder away from the group, we don't want another run in with the Deltas today."

The rest of the day went great; the group had visited almost every store they could find. They decided to visit the open-air markets and pick up some fresh fruit to take back with them. Mouse decided to stay close to the group and did not take any personal tours anywhere.

While in the market Ssam strolled, away to look at some boots he had seen. While looking at the boots he saw Dargon talking to two tall bearded strangers, both had tattoos of dragons on their left arms, red dragons. He watches them as long as he could while trying to hear what they were saying. He was wondering why Dargon was talking to them.

The rest of the group caught up with Ssam as Dargon and the two men separated and went in two different directions. "We have to be leaving," said Ssophia, "we need to get back to meet the professor." They all made their way to the land shuttle station and caught the first shuttle they could, that was leaving for the docking port.

CHAPTER 14

The Red Dragons and the Pirate War

Once reaching the port, they saw Professor Kai talking with Professor EaHaci. Everyone quickly made their way through the Control Center and back to their ship. Once they had reached the ship, Ssam begin telling everyone what he had seen. He told them about Dargon talking to the two strangers, with tattoos of red dragons on their left arms. Clair had been listening and gasped as he mentioned the tattoos, "The Red Dragons! They were supposed to have all been wiped out in the Pirate war."

Caalin looked at her "What was the pirate war?" Clair explained, "It happened long before any of us were born. When the Alliance was first established there were groups that opposed it. Most of these groups became pirates and begin attacking, looting and destroying any ship with Alliance symbols on them. The Alliance sent out battles ships and cruisers to defend alliance space. They patrolled the areas known for pirate activity. The pirates got bold, attacked the Cruiser Zentaron, and destroyed it. The destruction of the Zentaron was what started the War. The Alliance then sent its armada on a search and destroy mission, looking for any pirate ship or strong holds. The Headmaster was in the war, he might be able to tell you more about it."

Thomas Hall one of the upper classmen from Charlie Squadron, over heard them talking about the pirate war and told them. "My father lost his left arm in that war. He was an engineering officer on the Battle Ship Phantom, and received his injured when a missile destroyed the plasma-gas release ducts, which caused the plasma engine to explode." He continued, "They lost fifteen members of his engineering crew that day, and he now has a bionic arm, but it does not stop the nightmares he has from the war. My mother says he still wakes during the night with cold sweats."

The Pirate war was the talk of everyone during the flight back to school. No one noticed they had gone to dimensional drive or that they had landed at the school. It wasn't until Professor Kai came back from the front of the ship and said it was time to disembark that they knew they were even on the ground.

Once leaving the ship they hurried back to the dorms to drop off all the items they bought while in Parinta`. After dropping their items, everyone made their way to the dining hall for dinner. During dinner, the talk about the pirate war was still going on amongst the freshman class. It seemed the Red Dragons were the worst of the worst when it came to the pirates. If a Red Dragon ship attacked, they did not stop until they either destroyed the ship they attacked or were nearly destroyed themselves. No one captured by the Red Dragons were ever found alive or in one piece. Caalin decided that he would talk to the headmaster about this to see what he could tell him about the war.

After dinner, Caalin went down to the administration office to make an appointment to see the headmaster. Ms Serinora was on duty when he arrived and the only one in the office, she was a very attractive young woman with brown hair and bright blue eyes. Caalin, trying to be as formal as he could be while, requesting an appointment to speak with the headmaster. Ms Serinora smiled and asked, "Can you tell me the reason for your request?" Caalin tried to think fast and said, "Its research for our Politics and Policy class." Ms Serinora then replied, "I will check the headmasters schedule and will send you word of the time the headmaster can meet with you." Caalin thanked her and turned to walk out. As he reached the door Ms Serinora said, "Caalin next time you don't have to be so formal and hopefully you will have more time to stay and talk." Caalin seemed to blush as he quickly exited the room.

When Caalin returned to the dorm, everyone asked if he had gotten and appointment. He told them, "Ms Serinora said she would check the headmaster's schedule and would send him word on the time they could meet." He also told Ssam and Mouse what she said as he was walking out. Ang over heard the comment and in an angry tone snapped, "She was flirting with you! Why would she flirt with you?" Caalin replied, "She was just being friendly and was not flirting with me." Ang then turned and walked away toward her room and Ssophia quickly followed. After they had left the room Ssam looked at Caalin and said, "She was flirting with you wasn't she?" Caalin smiled, "Yes, but I wasn't going to admit it to Ang." The boys broke out into laughter.

The next morning everything was going normally, after breakfast they made their way to Universal history. After Professor Taran had taken his seat, Caalin raised his hand to ask a question. The professor looked at him, "Yes Mister Matthews?" Caalin then asked him, "Professor Taran can you tell us about the pirate war?" The rest of the students nodded their heads as to agree with Caalin, everyone but Dargon who seemed disinterested in the discussion. The Professor thought for a moment, "We were not supposed to get to the pirate war for another couple of weeks but since you seemed to be so interested, we can touch on it now."

He started, "The pirate war started thirty years ago when a pirate ship called Dragons Breath of the Red Dragon Clan destroyed an Alliance Cruiser Zentaron carrying diplomats to a conference on Eantheola. The Alliance issued orders to search down and capture or destroy the Dragons Breath. That was just the beginning; the pirates unleashed an all out attack order for Alliance ships and any ship doing business with the Alliance. The Alliance then deployed every ship it had available to go after the pirates. The commander of the Alliance Armada was Julius Horatio Matthews; and yes, he was Mister Matthew's Grandfather."

Dargon made the comment, "Another Matthews trying to make his mark in history at everyone else's expense." Caalin ignored the comment and continued to listen. The Professor was continuing and also ignoring what Dargon had said.

Continuing "He deployed the ships into four squadrons, which are the same squadron identifications we use here at the school. Their mission was to search down and capture or destroy pirate vessels and strong holds. The war was harsh and long because the pirates fought until the death when they thought they had no choice. The Alliance captured very few of the pirates so we got very little information on locations of strong holds or ships." Before Professor Taran could discuss, the war in any more detail the class period was over and everyone had to move on to their next class.

The professor told them, "We will continue with the topic in tomorrow's class." Dargon made a comment as they were leaving the classroom to his group, "It looks like another wasted day tomorrow as well." Caalin again paid his comment no attention and continued on to Engineering.

Engineering class went by with everyone working on plasma inductors and still talking about the war. Everyone seemed to have a story about a member of his or her family that was in the war. Clair Tilone's uncle died in an attack on a pirate strong hold on Wailonia, he was a Space Marine and the landing shuttle he was on had been shot down entering the atmosphere. Asgaya Gigagei's father received injuries in the battle of Khetaron when his skip fighter went down. He was air lifted out by the Space Marines that he had been supporting on the ground. Ric Harset said that he had heard that Dargon's family had a connection to the pirates and that his grandfather was actually the head of the Red Dragon Clan. He also heard that most of the Delta squadron was made up of people whose families where pirates or at the least dealt with them.

During Self-defense, there was no talk about the war. They spent entire class blocking and tossing each other around the room. Caalin was so distracted with everything going through his head that he forgot to block a blow from Devolon that sent him bouncing off a wall and left him breathless on the floor. Everyone looked over to see what had happened. Ang started toward him but he held out his hand to stop her. He told everyone, "I'm ok; I just lose my concentration and missed the block."

The Deltas just laugh and Dargon sneered, "He didn't miss the block Devolon was just better than Lord Matthews". Caalin just sneered back as he stood up "we will just see if he is or not." Just as he had gotten to his feet Devolon made a charge and Caalin quickly side stepped and threw him hard into the wall that he had the pleasure of meeting just a few seconds before. Professor Kai quickly called for everyone attention to stop what might have turned into a real fight. She assigned them three new moves to study that night and they would go over them the next day in class.

During lunch, Ang asked Caalin, "Are you really ok that bounce off the wall looked painful." Caalin told her, "I hoped the one I gave Devolon was just as painful." Ssophia look at Ang, "That is a boy's way of saying it hurt a lot." Mouse elbowed Ssam, "She's broken our code!" They all laughed at Mouse's remarks as the Deltas were setting at their table glaring over at them. Devolon leaned over to Dargon, "I'm going to get Matthews good tomorrow, and he won't be getting up so fast when I do." Dargon snapped back, "You won't do a thing; I have other plans for Lord Matthews." Devolon just growled, nodded his head yes and then began to eat his lunch staring and sneering in the Alpha direction.

CHAPTER 15

Meeting with the Headmaster

During lunch, Ra came over and gave Caalin a note from Ms Serinora. Caalin open the message and it read: *The headmaster will see you in his office tonight at eighteen hundred hours* then just below that *I look forward to seeing you again* and was signed Nesara. Nesara was Ms Serinora's first name and when Ang saw the message her face turned red with anger, but she did not say a word. The boys thought it was funny how just the mention of Ms Serinora's name would make Ang mad.

Politics and Diplomacy class went as it normally did, but when they reached Botany class Professor Ravin informed everyone they would now be studying the plants of Keeyontor. They would learn what plants are eatable, which ones were dangerous and which ones had medical properties.

Ssophia quickly held her hand up to ask a question, but before she could Professor Ravin intervened. "This is to prepare you for the Squadron Survival Tournament which will be held at the end of the semester." He continued to tell them, "The tournament is a one-week ordeal that will test your ability to navigate rough terrain, work as a team, and survive the elements."

He gave them handouts on all the plants on Keeyontor. It listed the plants as eatable, poisonous, carnivorous and medically helpful. The rest of the class period was spent going over how to tell the difference between the eatable berries and poisonous ones also covering eatable plants and plants that could eat them.

Their Geology class went pretty much the same as Botany, except Professor Grundor went over the different types of terrain features they would have to navigate. He covered the hazards everyone would encounter and the minerals useful for creating fires or explosions. They spent the class period going over all the elements they would find and how useful they could be.

During dinner, the talk had shifted from the pirate war to more about the tournament and wondering what it would be like. Questions like would it be squadron again squadron? How dangerous would it really be? No one seemed to have the answers to any of these questions and none of the upper classmates would give them any information about the tournament. One of the second year girls commented they would find out more later, so they should not be making such a big deal out of it.

In Language Professor Qua Chai covered the different languages they would encounter. All the clues and instructions they would receive would be in the form of a different written language. They would have to decide which language it is and decipher it for the information in order to move ahead in the challenge. The tournament would start out by dropping each squad in a different location they would have to first the clue container. In the container they would find instructions that they would have to decipher to find out where to go from there. Professor Qua Chai gave them one piece of information no one had mentioned. He informed them, "If you meet up with any of the other teams on the challenge, you have the option to team up to complete a challenge, but they had to follow all clues for each group, as long as their clues lead them in the same directions."

After class, everyone went back to their dorms still talking about the tournament. Caalin entered the common room and dropped his books on the main table, but just as he was about to set down Ssam reminded him, "You have your appointment with the headmaster." Due to all the talk about the tournament he had forgotten about the appointment and the information he wanted on the Red Dragons.

He quickly went to straighten his uniform, clean himself up, then out the door and off to the headmaster's office. As he entered the main office Ms Serinora met him with a smile, "Mr. Matthews how handsome you look this evening." Ms Teletora was standing behind her and turned around to face Caalin, "Oh, yes he does look very handsome today." Caalin smiled back a little red in the face, "I am here for my appointment with the headmaster." "Please go right in he is expecting you," replied Ms Serinora.

"Mr. Matthews how are you today and what do I owe the honor of meeting with you this evening?" asked the Headmaster. Caalin answered, "I am fine sir. I am hoping to ask you about the Pirate war and especially the about the Red Dragons."

Headmaster Keayan paused for a moment then told him to have a seat. Caalin sat down in the large chair in front of his desk. The headmaster stood in one spot for a few seconds then walked around the desk and set down on the corner of it. He told Caalin," If you want to know about the Pirate war I will first have to give you some background information that lead up to the war." He continued, "I have already told you about attending this very school with both your father and Dargon Drake's father and they were all good friends."

The headmaster continued, "We were always together and were all in the same squadron. We won the Skyracer race and the Survival Tournament, the same one in which you will soon be competing in." They also won a lot more tournament that everyone would be competing in the next few years while at Boldoron. "If you look in the Trophy Case in the Grand Common Hall, you will see your father's name along with Talon Drake, Dargon's father on many of the trophies."

"After our graduation we all went directly into the military and server in the same command for a while," he continued. "Then after some time we all became commanders of our own ships." "When the Pirate war began your grandfather, call us all to command headquarters. He asked Talon to resign his commission and return to his home planet as an agent of the Alliances. He wanted Talon to infiltrate the Red Dragons because they were the worst of all the pirates. He was to feed the Alliance all the information he could gather. Talon reluctantly did what your grandfather asked and once he returned home it did not take him long to become a Red Dragon." The headmaster paused, "He sent lots of useful information to us and save many lives by doing so. He even became a commander of his on ship as a Red Dragon. It was at the Battle of Delvar when your father's ship and mine came into conflict with Talon's ship. We had to make it look like a real battle pretending to keep his ship from escaping. We both fired shots over his bow and some that barely clipped his wings. We were trying to get as close as we could without doing much damage. This was to give him a chance to maneuver out and use his dimensional jump engines."

"Everything was going fine until your father's ship fired a missile and at the same time took a hit from a pirate skipfighter's lasers. The missile from your father's ship went off course and hit Talon's ship just as they went to Dimensional jump. There was a brighter flash of light than normal for dimensional jump and we thought we destroyed the pirate ship."

"We never heard anything from Talon again and your father never got over the thought of killing his friend. Your father resigned his commission after the war and went back into civilian life. I came here to teach and later became the headmaster. We thought we lose a great friend that day. It wasn't until I received the request for Dargon's enrollment here that I found out that Talon was still alive."

"From what information I have gathered, the explosion caused severe injuries and he spent the rest of the war recovering in a hospital. Dargon's mother was his nurse and the daughter of the Red Dragon Clan's Chief. I have been trying to find out more but he has not responded to any of my correspondences. Now what is your interest in the Pirate War and the Red Dragons?" he asked.

Caalin paused for a moment still taking in all the information that he had just received. "Well sir when we were in Parinta` Ssam saw Dargon talking to two men and both had red dragon tattoos on their left arms. Are there still some of the Red Dragon Pirates around?"

The headmaster thought for a moment saying nothing. He then rose off his desk, "I don't know Caalin, I don't think we destroyed them all in the war, but I cannot conceive that any of them would show their selves in Parinta`." Then he paused again, "I will send word to the Alliance Council to have this issue looked into, I'll assure you that there is nothing to worry about while here at school or while you're with any of the professors." He paused for one last time, "Do you have any further questions that you would like to ask?"

Caalin told him, "Not at this time sir, but can I request another meeting if I think of anything that I may have missed?" The headmaster laughed, "Anytime you have any questions feel free to request a meeting." With that he escorted Caalin to the door and told him, "Have a good night's sleep, you will need all the rest you can get between now and the end of the semester." As Caalin walked back through the main office both Ms Serinora and Ms Teletora smiled at him and told him to have a good evening.

It was late when Caalin got back to the dorm and no one was wake. He quickly got ready for bed and crawled in. Just as soon as he put his head down he heard Mouse say, "We will want a full report on your meeting tomorrow so get some sleep." Caalin smiled at the comment and drifted off to sleep.

The next day at breakfast the questions were flying at Caalin like laser blasts. He was finally able to stop them by telling everyone to set down, be quite and he would tell them everything he and the headmaster had discussed. Everyone settled down and was hanging on every word as Caalin filled them in between bites of food. He was hungry and was not going to let telling the group what he knew stop him from eating.

He went through everything the headmaster told him about the war, and Dargon's father. He also told them he had informed the headmaster about the two men with the Red Dragon tattoos Ssam had seen on Parinta'. The headmaster was going to pass the information along to the Alliance Council to look into. By the time Caalin had finish talking it was time for class and he was the only one that had finished breakfast, everyone else had been so busy listening they forgot to eat. They all grabbed what they could to eat on the way to class so as not to starve before lunch. As they walked to their class, Ssam told Caalin, "I can't believe that your father was best friends with Dargon's father."

In History class, Professor Taran began to teach the history of Keeyontor. He discussed what the settlers of Keeyontor were like. Most of the planets population was miners that mined for Goran Crystals, precious stones used in fusion reactors. It was a hard life at first but over a period of time businesses sprung up around the mining industry. The planet then became a thriving republic whose mining business slowly faded with the mining of less and less crystals. The planet by then had became a trade world and built the infrastructure around interplanetary trading. Keeyontor has mountains, deserts and rich green jungles that during the tournament they would have to maneuver. The entire history class was now devoted to Keeyontor and its people.

In engineering class, Professor Marru was now covering thing they could constructed out of parts they could find in and around some of the old abandon mines. He pulled out several bins of parts from a storage area. "These are the type of things you will find around the old mining areas," he told them. The class covered how to build communicators and simple two-way walkie-talkie like devices they could use in communicating with each other in case of emergencies. They went over how to build global positioning devices that would help them in navigation. After going over everything they began using the parts in the bins to build the items they had discussed. The last part of the class period was spent trying to build a simple communications device, but none of the devices worked properly.

In Self-defense Professor Kai took them to a large hanger behind the classroom where there was a large rock-climbing wall. She turned to the class and looked over at Ang, "Not all of you have the ability to fly so you will need to work on your climbing skills. Even those people that can fly should also work on their climbing. You never know what could happen that would keep you from being able to take flight." Ang smiled back at the professor then joined in with the rest of the class.

The Deltas seemed to make it into a contest every time someone started up the wall. Caalin held back with his abilities, which seem to allow him to defy gravity, so as not to let the Deltas know what he could do. When Devolon beat Caalin up the wall Mouse look at him in discuss, "You could have left him in your dust!" Caalin smiled, "I know but I didn't want them to know I can." Class went on one race after another, boys against boys, girls against girls and girls against boys. The girls from both groups bonded a little when they were competing against the boys. Ang and Ssophia found that Evalon and Keyan were not as bad as they thought, even though they were part of Delta Squadron. The boys did not fare as well; they still did not get along at all.

During lunch, the girls from Alpha and Delta set together and talked. They even had the girls from Beta and Charlie squads join them, and it seemed that all of the girls got along very well. The boys could not believe that the girls would fraternize with the Delta girls. Caalin wondered if the

Delta girls were doing it to get information from them. If they were what kind of information were they looking for?

In Politics and Diplomacy, they covered the different laws they would have to follow while on Keeyontor. They covered the thing they could do and those they could not do while on the planet. They covered the customs of the different groups of people that lived there. If it was part of the planets laws or customs they seem to be covering it.

When they got to their Botany class Professor Ravin had bowls and bowls of different eatable plants. Now they would have the chance to see what they looked like and taste like. They spent the class feeling, smelling and tasting the different plants. Some of them tasted awful and others tasted great. The Professor told them that unfortunately in the wilderness they would find more of the awful tasting ones than the good tasting ones.

In Geology class, they spent time going over three-dimensional maps of the planet. They learned how to recognize terrain features to find water and shelter. Under what type of rocks they could find eatable insect and lizards, how to tell if an area was prone to rock slides. They learned how to tell if a cave was safe to enter or not, and at the end of class they had a lot of material to go over on the planets desert and mountain areas.

Finally, in Language class they were doing the same old thing, going over the different languages they would find on the planet. Professor Qua Chai gave them a list of phrases and words they had to translate. In addition at the end of class he gave them a stack of words and phrases he would test them on the next day.

At dinner the girls from all four squadrons sat at one table together talking, Caalin and Ssam were going over the language papers, and Mouse was looking over some technical designs for communicators. None of them were eating very much; it seemed that the plants they had sampled earlier had stuck with them. Mouse finally found a simple but effective communication system and quickly moved over to show it to Caalin and Ssam. They decided when they got back to the dorm they could check them out on the computer and test the design by running some simulations.

Once back in the dorm common area the boys quickly got on one of the computers, putting in all of the communicator information on the system and brought up the specifications. It was a simple two-way system with a range of about five kilometers. They verified that it would work well enough to communicate with each other on the planet. They printed off the parts list so they would be able to look for the parts they needed. Their next task was to find a global positioning system they could build with ease.

The girls finally returned to the dorm from dinner and everyone sat down at the large table in the common area and began going over the words and phrases they needed to know for language class the next day. They would argue over the punctuation and meaning of them as they studied. They would laugh at each other when one of them would pronounce a word wrong. One phrase Ssam had mispronounced that was supposed to mean, could you help me please, came out as could I smell your feet. After a couple of hours of this everyone shuffled off to bed.

The next day classes continued to cover the things they would need to know for the challenge. In engineering, the boys used their list to find the parts they needed to build the communicators. They shared their list with the Beta boys and all of them worked together building the communicators. By the end of the class period, they had six working units. Each group had three units but all of them were on the same frequency. Now their task was to find out how to change the frequencies on the systems so they could communicate between each other without having their conversations over heard.

The rest of the day went as usual. In language class, they had their test, and the boys worried about whether or not they passed it. However, during dinner Professor Zento made an announcement. The third day of the following week was family visitation day for the parents, grandparents, brothers, sisters or any relative that had part in the student's upbringing. "We have informed your families of this date and they will be letting the school know who will be visiting from each your families. You will know by the end of the week what family members will be coming for the day." This information changed the conversation from the tournament to the visitation day. Everyone was now talking about who might be coming from his or her family and they had three days to wonder about it.

In the dorm, Ang asked Caalin, "Do you think your parents will be coming, I would like to meet them. I think mine might come or at lease my mother and Mouse's mother, but I hoped both my parents make it." Ssam said, "It will probably be our parents and grandmother. She goes everywhere with them when it pertains to her grandchildren. She hated it when they sent us off to school." "Nam loves us dearly," said Ssophia "and I really miss her." "Me too" concluded Ssam in a low soft voice. Mouse said, "I hope my father comes I wanted to show him our racer in the engineering bay."

Excitement was high the rest of the week with everyone hoping to find out who was coming to visit. Finally the end of the week was here that morning at breakfast it was all that was talked about amongst the students, but they would not know until the end of the day. They would each find a letter with the information in their dorm room that evening; therefore everyone had to make it through what seemed to be the longest day of classes. Every class seemed to drag on longer than it should, and lunch seemed to go by faster since everyone was discussing what the evening was going to bring.

That evening before dinner, Ang and Ssophia went by their dorm but there was not any letters on the table, so disappointed they went to the dining hall to meet the boys. As they entered the dining hall Mouse looked up at Ang with excitement but that died quickly when she shook her head no. Caalin say that the letters would probably be there when they returned after dinner the delivery is probably going on now. Everyone agreed with him and decided to enjoy their dinner. After dinner everyone hurried back to the room and sure enough, as Caalin had predicted, the letters were lying on the table.

CHAPTER 16

Skiffer Racing

Everyone opened the letters with excitement, reading them as fast as possible, to find out that everyone's parents were coming including Ssophia and Ssam's Nam. This really made everyone's day; they could not wait to tell all their friends. Ssophia and Ang quickly left to go tell all the girls and as they hurried down the hallway they ran into Evalon and Keyan and told them. Evalon's mother and grandmother were coming her father was away on business. Keyan's father and grandfather were coming her mother was sick and her grandmother was staying back to take care of her. The girls made their rounds to visit both the Beta and Charlie dorms. In the Beta dorm, they found out that Clair Tilone and Asgaya Gigagei had both their parents coming. Sisten Waron's mother and grandparents were coming her father had died the year before she came to Boldoron; he was killed test piloting a new skipfighter. He had emerged from a dimensional jump right into an asteroid field and did not have time to avoid a collision because his jump sensors failed to function properly giving him no warning...

After leaving the Beta dorm, they went straight to see the girls in Charlie squadron. Mari Ekahau, Patrish Aningan and Atira Estanatlehi had both their parent coming. Mari's younger brother was also coming and he would probably be attending the school next year.

The boys did not run from dorm room to dorm room, they just all gathered in the large commons room and shared their information. The Beta boys, Ric Harset and Marty Jiison had both their parents coming. Jason Rogers of Charlie squadron had his father and grandfather coming; his mother was staying home with his two younger sisters. Gahe Gluskap also of Charlie squadron had his father, mother and sister coming. The Delta squadron boys were not around but no one seemed to wonder about who was coming to visit them.

The girls all talked had talked with the Delta girls and informed the boys that both of Dargon's parents would be coming. This made Caalin wonder what was going to happen, the headmaster said they have not heard from Dargon's father since the Pirate war not until Dargon came to the academy. It seemed that Devolon's father would be coming but no one else from his family, his mother would be staying at home with his three brothers and four sisters. Jon Cizin however had both his parents and both his brothers attending. The boys filled the girls in with the information they had so by the time they all went to bed everyone knew who was coming from everyone's families.

The next two days were off days so everyone had the time to rest. The boys decided they would have skiffer races and would meet outside of the engineering classroom. Not everyone had a skiffer so they would use the skiffers that some of the boys had brought from home. Mouse had one stashed away in his gear and quickly pulled it out before heading down to engineering. They quickly set up a course outside of engineering in the area behind the hanger, which consisted of ramps, jumps and two tunnels made from thruster tubes. You had to weave through the obstacles, up one side of the ramps and down the other, make the jumps then through the tunnels and across the finish line. Mouse explained how to use the skiffer to some of the boys that had never seen one. "You use your weight to stir the board, shifting it right or left to change direction and back and forth to make it go up or down," he explained. The fun part was watching Mouse's trainees using the boards for the first time. They were crashing and falling into everything.

Ric Harset was the first one to challenge Caalin to a race. They both mounted the boards at the starting line as Mouse counted down to start the race "3, 2, 1, Go!" They were off and ran head to head as they made their way through the obstacles. They went up and down the ramp, and over the jumps. When they turned to go through the tunnels Caalin push his skiffer forward and took a small lead beating Ric across the finish line by centimeters.

Gahe looked over at Mouse and told him it was his turn to lose. Mouse grabbed his board and met him at the starting line. Ric counted down the start and yelled go and they were off. Mouse maneuvered the obstacle so quickly it stunned everyone. When he hit the ramp he did a back flip as he reached the top then landed and flew down the other side. As he made the jumps he completed three spins in midair. Entering the tunnel he made loops as he came through, and to add insult to injury he beat Gahe by at least two meters. When he crossed the finish line everyone met him cheering and talking about how awesome his run was, even Gahe was impressed. Mouse admitted that he had been riding skiffers for so long it felt like an extension of his body.

While everyone was talking to Mouse about his run a voice from behind the group said, "I will take him on." It was Dargon and his two goons Jon and Devolon. Mouse accepted the challenge and they both met at the starting line. Gahe counted down the start and they were off. They stayed close through the obstacles, at the ramp Dargon was a few inches ahead, but when they got to the jumps Mouse had caught up with him. They made the turn for the tunnels and as they were getting close Dargon gave Mouse a push crashing him into the side of the tunnel. His skiffer went one way and he went the other. As Dargon crossed the finish line he stopped and looked back at Mouse, "It looks like someone lost part of his body." Then he and his two goons walked off laughing.

Mouse got up furious, he was ok, but skiffer had some damaged from hitting the edge of the tunnel. Caalin told Mouse to calm down Dargon would get his eventually. Mouse made some repairs to his skiffer in the engineering classroom then his way back to the races. They continued to race each other until lunch. Making their way to the dining hall everyone continued to talk about the things Mouse could do on a skiffer.

At lunch, the boys met up with the girls and Ssam filled them everything they had been doing. He told them about the skiffer course they lay out and all the races they had ran. When he told them about the race between Mouse and Dargon and what had happen the girls were infuriated. Ssophia told them she was ready to go over to the Delta table and give him a piece of her mind. The boys' calmed her down and told her they would get even with him, they just needed a plan. Ssam stated, "Besides you can't spare any of your mind you barely have enough as it is." Ssophia hit him on the shoulder and gave him a nasty look as everyone laughed.

They continued eating their lunch and talking about the races. Then Caalin said, "L have an idea, if we continued to have our races this afternoon Dargon would surely show up again and that would give us the opportunity to give him the surprise of his life." He explained, "First, we needed Ssam to sneak into the Medical wing and get some rubber gloves. Then we will fill the gloves with as much water as they will hold. Ssam and Ssophia will take two gloves filled with water and stand along the wall bending in with it." "Then" he smiled, "Ang will fly up to the top of the wall above everyone." The rest of the plan was that Caalin and Mouse would draw Dargon out with a challenge. Mouse would race him again and when Mouse beats Dargon, and he would this time, everyone will hit him with the gloves filled with water at the finish line. It was a great plan and the minute lunch was over Ssam left running off toward the Medical wing for gloves.

While Ssam was getting the gloves Mouse and Caalin gathered the Beta and Charlie boys together and filled them in on the plan. Everyone was excited at the idea of getting Dargon back for some of his stunts. Ssam made it back with a box of gloves and they quickly began to fill them with water. Once they were all outside at the skiffer course Ssam took his place along one wall and Ssophia took hers at the other wall. Ang took as many gloves as she could carry and flew up to the top of the wall behind them this left the rest of the group to lure Dargon out.

Jason Rogers decided to go find him and tell him that Caalin and Mouse said that he could not beat Mouse in a fair race if his life depended on it. When Jason got the word to Dargon, he turned red with anger. He growled "I can beat that runt with both hands behind my back," and he and his two goons rushed down to the course to prove it.

When he got there, everyone was racing so as not to let him catch on to what was up. Ssam and Ssophia had blended in with the wall behind them so he could not see them. Dargon quickly challenged Mouse to another race but Mouse declined saying in the last race almost destroyed his skiffer and it was not running properly. One of the other boys told Mouse he could use his skiffer and handed it to him. This had all been planned out before Dargon had arrived. Mouse said, "Ok, I'll race you", and they both took their position at the starting line.

Devolon quickly counted down the start and yelled go and Dargon took off with the led. Mouse quickly caught him and passed him. Mouse maintained his lead all the way to the end of the race not giving Dargon any chance to catch him. Everyone cheered as Mouse crossed the finish line. Dargon was out raged, "You got lucky you little runt, but your luck will soon run out." "It looks like your luck is what ran out!" shouted Caalin. Then Ssam, Ssophia and Ang began tossing the water gloves at him. He was quickly soaked with watered and the entire group laughed until their sides hurt. Dargon was furious and started toward Caalin with his fist ready, but when everyone moved forward to meet him, he stopped in his tracks. He turned to Devolon and Jon, told them let's go, and as they were leaving he looked back at Caalin, "You'll get yours Matthews just remember that!"

The boy's still laughing went back to their racing. Ang and Ssophia wondered off to meet the other girls and tell them what they did to Dargon. This was the talk of the day the rest of the afternoon. At dinner they would look over at the Delta table and chuckle thinking about how funny it was. After dinner everyone stayed in the dining hall playing board games and talking. That night it seemed like everyone had their best night's sleep since they had arrived at Boldoron.

The next morning Dargon was still the topic of many conversations as everyone seemed to be spending the day preparing their uniforms for the upcoming family visit. The boys made sure all their ribbons were on the uniforms and boots were polished. After their uniforms were ready the boys spent the rest of the day running more skiffer races and playing board games.

The next two days everyone was both excited and nervous about the family day ahead. They found it hard to concentrate on studies; even the Delta squad was having problems. Finally the day arrived; the families would be arriving at nine o'clock. Caalin put on his normal daily uniform that morning. Ssam looked at him and asked, "Why are you wearing your daily uniform and not the one you prepared for the visit?" Caalin answered, "I don't want to get anything on it at breakfast." Mouse and Ssam decided that was a great idea and they put on their daily uniform too.

CHAPTER 17

Family Visit

The boys were a little late for breakfast because Caalin had to wait on Ssam and Mouse to get dressed. When they got to the dining hall the girls were shocked to see them in the daily uniform and everyone else in the dress uniforms. Caalin was just about to explain to the girls why they were dressed in their everyday uniform when Marty Jiison spilled his drink in his lap. Caalin just pointed over to him and said to the girls, "That is why we didn't wear our good uniforms." They were all laughing at the thought of one of them doing the very same thing when Mouse knocked his drink over onto Ssam. Everyone laughed even harder at the site of Ssam jumping up and trying to brush off the liquid, getting most of it back on Mouse. Ssophia stated, "That was a great idea since you boys are so clumsy." Mouse looked at the girls with a funny expression on his face, "Hey we represent that remark" and they all broke into laughter again.

After breakfast the boys ran back to the dorm and quickly changed into their fresh uniforms and scurried back to meet the girls. Everyone was in the dining hall with the Squadron Advisors when the boys arrived. Professor Taran was going over the procedures for the arrival of the families. The families would be arriving in shuttles designated for each squadron. Alpha's family would be arriving at docking port one, Beta at two, Charlie at three and Delta at four. After you meet your family you will show them around and then escort them back to the dining hall at noon. They will be served lunch and meet the school staff at that time. He then said, "You may go ahead and make your way to the docking ports."

Everyone rushed down to the docking ports and waited for the shuttles to arrive. As the shuttles began arriving the excitement intensified while waiting for the doors to open and their families to disembark. As the families came through the doors the students rush to greet them. Ssam and Ssophia's family was the first off the shuttle and the group knew right off whose parents they were, the family resemblance was uncanny. Then there were Ang and the Mouse's parents who had traveled together. Both of Ang's parents had wings and her mother was beautiful Caalin could see where Ang got her looks. Caalin looked at Mouse's parents and Mouse looked just like his dad but his mother, who was Ang's aunt, was also as beautiful as Ang's mother but did not have wings. Caalin turned to Ang to ask her why but before he could say a word she said, "Not all Averiaerans are born with wings". Caalin looked as if she had read his mind. Then finally, Caalin's Parent came walking through the door, and Caalin rush to greet them. His mother met him with open arms as hugs and kisses passed between them all.

Caalin's father then told him, "I will have to catch up with you later; I have a meeting scheduled with the headmaster so I will see you in the dining hall at noon." Caalin ask, "Do you need me to show you the way to the office?" His father smile, "I think I can remember where it is, but thanks for offering." Caalin's Mother said, "He should know where it is, he spent a lot of time there when he was here." Caalin's father looked at her with a smile, "Now dear it wasn't always for something I did." The group broke into laughter. As he was walking away, he told Caalin, "Give your mother the grand tour and don't leave anything out."

After he was out of sight Caalin and the others started introducing the families. Mouse's father informed them that the parents had already introduced themselves on the shuttle, so all they needed to do is introduced them to their friends. Everyone tried to introduce Caalin to their family at the same time but it was so confusing the Ang's father took over and did the honors. He told Caalin, "Ang, had written fondly of you", this made Caalin turn a bright red. Then he asks that everyone introduce themselves to the family members, one at a time.

After the students had introduced themselves, the family members then introduced their selves to the students. After the introductions Jillian, Caalin's mother went over to Ang and told her that she appreciated how Ang had rescued Caalin after the skyracer crash. She continued, "Caalin has written us about the entire incident and that he really is fond of you too." Ang thanked her as she blushed with the thought that Caalin made it a point to tell his parents about her. She looked over at Caalin and gave him a smile causing him to turn red again.

Mouse was excited to show his parents the skyracer so the rest of the group appointed him the official tour guide. The first place he took everyone was straight to engineering. Where they ran into the Beta squad and everyone went through introductions again. After the introductions, that seemed to take too long for Mouse's taste, he rushed everyone over to the racer.

He pointed out every little detail from the engine design to the cockpit layout. Caalin's mother leaned over to Ang and asked, "Is he always this way?" She smiled, "only when it comes to rockets, gadgets and electronics, he doesn't get this excited about any of the other schoolwork." They both laughed and Caalin looked around at them to see what was so funny and they quickly put on straight faces. Then when he turned back around, they both giggled again and he just shook his head.

After they left engineering they made their way toward the dorm room. On the way there they ran into the Delta group in the hallway. The girls of both groups began to introduce everyone since the boys did not seem to care too. When the girls introduced Dargon's mother Caalin notice she was an attractive woman, very quiet, and not at all like Dargon. She told everyone that Dargon's father would be joining them later he had a meeting with the headmaster. This stunned Caalin and sent him wondering what they were doing, what were they discussing. Did his father know that Dargon's father was alive?

When they reached the dorm they showed their parents their rooms. This was the first time the boys had ever been in the girl's room. It was similar to theirs but the girls had decorated it with what Mouse called girly things. They had fancy blankets with ruffled edges and the women in the group seemed to like the way it was decorated. Then when the girls went into the boy's room Sophia said, "I knew the walls would covered with pictures of spaceships, rockets and their designs." The boys had plain grey blankets and their lockers were a disorderly mess. Nam said. "The boys need the girls to give them some lessons on organization it would make things easier to find in their lockers." The girls giggle at the thought of them helping the boys.

When everyone had finished in the dorm room it was time to make their way to the dining hall. On their way there they ran into the Charlie squad and went through a completely new set of introductions. They met Jason's father and grandfather, plus both Patrish and Atira's father and mother. Then they met Mari's father, mother and little brother, who seemed to be a little brat and love to terrorize people, and finally, Gahe's father, mother and cute little sister, that Mari's brother seem to be terrorizing at that particular moment. As they all turned and walked toward the dining hall Caalin leaned over and told Mari's brother. "there are cameras everywhere and if you kept being mean to Gahe's sister there was no telling what they may put in his food. " Mari's brother suddenly became very polite and quickly apologized for his behavior. Mari whispered to Caalin, "I don't know what you said to him but thanks pal I owe you big time." Caalin just smiled and said it was nothing. Ang hear the conversation and turned and gave him another smile and he went crimson red again.

CHAPTER 18

The Meeting

While the tours were going on throughout the school Talon and Thomas, Dargon and Caalin's fathers were enroot to meet with the headmaster. Talon arrived just a few moments ahead of Thomas, as he entered the headmaster's office, headmaster Keayan turned to greet him, "Talon, it is great to see you my old friend." Talon looked at him without a smile on his face, "Nathaniel I can't say that I hold the same feelings." Before they could go any further with their conversation, Thomas entered the room. The moment he saw Talon his eyes looked like they were about to pop out of his head, "Talon I thought you were dead!" Talon, with anger in his eyes, snapped back, "I should have been since my friends tried to kill me!" "What do you mean", asked Thomas? "Don't you remember how you shot my ship as we were entering a dimensional jump? We were barely able to get into the escape pods before the ship exploded! My pod was trapped for five days inside the dimensional rip. It wasn't until a pirate ship jumping through pulled my pod out in its wake. Once I was out of the rip they were able to pick up my signal and rescue me" he explained. He gave them the coordinates he was using when entering into the dimensional jump before ship took a hit; so they were able to rescue what was left of his crew.

Thomas replied," Talon your wrong we did not mean to hit your ship. We had locked in a path that would miss your ship by meters." He continued, "Just as we fired the missiles we took a hit ourselves from a pirate skipfighter. That explosion altered our position and caused the missiles to go off course and hit your ship." "I left the military after the war because I couldn't live with the thought of having killed one of my best friends. If you don't believe me ask Nathaniel to show you the record of the incident in the archive." He ended by saying, "you are one of my dearest and most trusted friends and I have missed you."

"He is right Talon, and I can show you the files to prove it," said Nathaniel. There was a long silence between the men then Nathaniel broke it by saying, "You two were unbearable while in school. You were always going after the cutest girls and never gave me a break." Talon just stood there not smiling not saying a word, then all of a sudden broke into laughter, "When you're right Nathan, you're right." He and Thomas then grabbed each other in a big hug and Nathan joined in by grabbing them both.

Nathan reminded them about how they use to chase the girls while in school and was always seeing two or three different girls at the same time. Talon said, "I couldn't believe the girls never caught on, if they had they would have killed us both." He then asked Thomas "whatever happened to the skinny little girl you were seeing before we graduated." Thomas looked at him with a straight face, "I married her." They all laughed and Thomas told him about how he had corresponded with her during and after the war, she had consoled him on the losing his friend. They fell in love got married and had a son. "Now let's hear about you," Thomas said, "what happened after you were rescued?"

Talon told them," my injuries were so bad I spent months in the hospital, and almost a year in rehab learning to walk again. While in rehab I met my wife, she was my rehab nurse. She pushed me so hard while I was in rehab that I had to fall in love with her. We have a son also; we named him Dargon that was Monique's maiden name. It turned out that her father was Remus Dargon the former leader of the Red Dragons."

Both Thomas and Nathan had a surprised look on their faces. Thomas jumped in, "you are married to the daughter of the Red Dragons leader." Talon replied, "Former leader, he left the Red Dragons before the war was over, he wanted to make peace with the Alliance and the rest of the pirates were no in favor of it. That is when he stepped down."

Nathan interrupted at that point to tell them, "That is why I asked for this meeting. One of the students saw two men with Red Dragon tattoos on their arms while they were on Parinta`." He then asked Talon, Have you heard anything about the Red Dragons coming out of hiding?" Talon said, "I've heard some rumors but nothing that I can confirm. I heard something big was going down but I don't know what, when or where."

Nathan told them both, "I think it might be something involving the school or some of the students, so I will need your help. Talon I need you to keep your eyes and ears open for any talk about anything that may involve the school or students. Thomas, can you talk to the Alliance Council about providing security for the upcoming survival tournament?" He said, "This has to stay a secret and no one else outside this room should be told anything, not even your wives."

Nathan looked at his watch, "It Looks like it's time for you to rejoin your families." As they were leaving his office he said, "I should also let you know that your sons are not the best of friends like you were, in fact they don't get along at all." Talon looked back at him "Neither did we our first year remember." Then he and Thomas walked out of the office laughing.

CHAPTER 19

Return to the Family

Talon and Thomas caught up with their families in the dining hall where Caalin quickly took his father around and introduced him to everyone. It was a big surprise to Dargon to find out that his father knew Caalin's father, but it did not change his attitude toward Caalin at all. It was an even bigger surprise to Caalin that his mother new Dargon's father and had went to school with them. Neither his mother nor father had told him she had attended school here.

Talon looked at her smiling, "Jillian you're not the skinny little girl I remember Thomas and I teasing, you've turned into a very lovely woman." Jillian blushed, "Thank you for the compliment though I still haven't forgot the stink bomb the two of you threw into our dorm room." Talon and Thomas laughed at the image of the dorm room emptying into the hallway because of the smell and the trouble they got into with the headmaster over it. Then Jillian looked over to Monique, "They were always into mischief and trouble if it had not been that the headmaster thought fondly of the two of them I think they would have been expelled their first year."

Thomas told Jillian, "you should stop with the stories in front of the students they may get ideas that Nathan wouldn't be happy about.' Jillian looked at Thomas with surprise, "You mean Nathaniel Keayan is the headmaster?" Talon jumped in, "Yes can you believe it, he was the worst of us all." Their laughter came to a halt when Headmaster Keayan and the staff entered the room.

As the staff made their way into the room and to their seats, the students and their families took their seats. Headmaster Keayan told everyone how great it was that the families could find the time to visit the school and he hoped that they were enjoying their visit. He introduced himself for those that did not know him and then introduced his staff. He also informed them that he and his staff would be available after lunch for any questions the family members might have about the school or how their sons or daughters were doing. He then said, "I hope everyone enjoys their meal, but remember that the shuttles will be leaving promptly at sixteen hundred hours."

Everyone enjoyed the food and afterward began to mingle again. Caalin took his father down to engineering to show him the racer that he had missed seeing earlier. While they were in engineering, he asked his father why he had not told him that he knew the headmaster. Thomas said, "Honestly son I didn't know that Nathaniel was the headmaster here." He then told Caalin that Talon, Nathaniel and he were the closest of friends while he went to school here. He said, "It was at this very school where I met your mother. However, it was not until after the war that I really fell in love with her." He also told Caalin how the three of them use to see how much mischief they could cause for the headmaster. He thought that the fact the headmaster at that time was a dear close friend of his grandfather is the only reason he did not have them expelled.

Caalin's mother and the rest of his group caught up with them in engineering. The students then took the families down the halls to visit the other classrooms. As the group entered the self-defense classroom Professor Kai looked up from her desk then quick jumped to her feet. As she came around her desk she looked at Caalin's mother, "Jillian it's been so long since I've seen you." Jillian quickly went to hug her, "Marjori I didn't know you were teaching here." Marjori looked over at Thomas, "I see you finally got Matthews to pay attention to you." They both laughed at the comment and Jillian told her not to talk to loud he did not know about her trying so hard to catch him while they were in school. Thomas walked over and ask them what was so funny and the two of them said at the same time, "Oh nothing" then laughed again. Thomas said, "You girls have not changed at all since school." They broke into even more laughter.

All the women in the group gathered around Marjori and Jillian and where having a big conversation about their husbands. Jillian seemed to be talking to Ang off to the side and they would constantly look over at Caalin and giggle. The boys move to the mats and were demonstrating some of their moves and throws for the men in the group. Mouse's father showed the boys a move he used when he was in school. Ang's father made the comment, "the girls love to watch him do it."

He would act as if he was walking away then do three back flips with a spinning kick at the end. Caalin tried the move and nailed it on the first attempt this impressed Ang's father. He told Caalin, "Victor and I were in school Victor was the only person I knew who could do that move. Moreover, Victor took six weeks to master the move the first time." Ssam and Mouse both attempted it and landed flat on their faces. This gave Caalin and the others got a good laugh.

Time was slowly running out for the visit so everyone started moving back toward the docking ports. As they were walking through the halls they bumped into Professor Qua Chai. It turned out that Alan, Ang's father knew him, "Shan you teach here too?" Professor Qua Chai looked at Alan, "Alan I haven't seen or heard from you since we served together on the Phoenix." Lord Avora turned and told everyone, "Shan was the communications officer on the Alliance Ship Phoenix during the Pirate War." Professor Qua Chai told them, "Alan was the security officer on the ship and we went on many landings together." Geanio, Ssam and Ssophia's father told them he was on the Alliance Ship Slayer as the logistics officer. Alan told Shan to walk with them on the way to the docking ports, as they did Thomas, Geanio, Shan and he all discussed their military careers with each other.

When they reach the port Thomas saw Talon about to board his shuttle and went to say good-bye. He and Talon hugged and shook hands, they promised to stay in better touch now that they understood what had happened. Dargon was not happy seeing his father so friendly with Caalin's father and just sneered at them while they were talking.

Thomas turned and returned to his group and said his good-byes to Caalin and the rest of the students. Jillian gave Caalin a big hug then turned and gave Ang a hug. As she was doing so she whispered something in Ang's ear that made her giggle. Ang then whispered to Ssophia and they both giggle. Ssophia gave Jillian a hug also and told her it was great meeting her. After the tearful good-byes everyone stood in the docking port until the shuttles had lifted off and disappeared through the clouds. Professor Qua Chai then turned to the students and told them it was nice meeting their parents and his old friend Lord Avora. Then he told them to be off with their selves they could find better things to do with the rest of their day than stand in the docking port staring out the blast window. Everyone moved slowly down the hallway back toward the dorms.

CHAPTER 20

The Survival Tournament Begins

Back in the dorm the group was discussing their parents and the interesting things they found out about them. Ang stated, "Caalin's mother was very nice." "Yes and we learned a lot of interesting things from her", replied Ssophia as they giggled. Caalin gave them a worried look wondering what his mother could have told them. They were all amazed that some of the parents knew some of the teachers. Mouse stated, "I could not believe that Caalin's and Dargon's father were such good friends." Ssam agreed, "But Dargon's father was very nice and not like Dargon at all." Caalin commented, "Dargon must be like his grandfather, I heard he was the leader of the Red Dragons during the war." "That would explain it", said Ang's "he has Red Dragon blood in him." Their conversations went on until dinner and continued while they walked to the dining hall. That evening after dinner they sat around in their dorm room playing board games and continuing to discuss the family visit.

The next morning everything was back to normal, the boys were running late for breakfast so Ang and Ssophia got their breakfast for them and had it at the table when they arrived in the dining hall. They had about fifteen minutes to eat the meal and then off to class. Classes were going the same, as before the visit, they were to prepare everyone for the upcoming survival tournament. Dargon seemed a little quieter than usual, as if he had something bothering him and he acted as if he did not want anyone to find out. Caalin, Ssam and Mouse were suspicious and decided to keep their eyes on him. They recruited the boys from the other squads to help in their efforts. However, for all their snooping no one found out any information as to what Dargon may or may not be up to.

In engineering class they were going up in shuttles and being dropped in landing pods to simulate the drop they would undergo on the starting day of the tournament. Professor Grundor explained, "There will be four different shuttles and they would drop the groups into different locations at the same time. Once on the ground you will have to do a search of their landing areas to find a crate that will have the equipment and information you will need. The information will be in a language that will need to be deciphered in order to get your direction for the first objective." He also stated, "If any of the other groups meet up you can share information and assist each other in any way you wish. The object is to get from the drop zone to the finish line first, but you will have to make several checkpoints along the way." He continued telling them the groups would only have seven days to complete the course and professors from the school and independent monitors from the Alliance Council would be monitoring every move using satellite surveillance. The record time for completion of the Tournament was five days and thirteen hours set by Thomas Matthews, Talon Drake, Nathaniel Keayan, Marri Jinsop and Tylor Randor. Caalin leaned over to the rest of his group and told, "We are going to do our best to set a new record." He wanted to break the one set by his father, the headmaster and the others in their group.

As the weeks before the tournament went on, the shuttle would drop the students further and further away from school. They had to decipher information they were given and find their way back to the school. Some of the teams took most of the day to get back others seemed to be able to do it in just a few hours. This gave them a chance to find out what their strong points and weak points were and who in their groups were best at solving problems they encountered. Some had problems with the translations and others with improvising devices to get the direction correct. Beta squad had to be picked up one evening because they had translated their information incorrectly and was moving in the opposite direction from the school.

Professor Qua Chai asked them were they planning to get back by walking around the planet.

It was the final days before the tournament. The landing pods were fitted with the items each squad could take with them once they were on the ground. There was one canteen per person that would hold enough water for a twenty-four hour period. They would have two large knives that they could us for cutting and one solar blanket per person. Anything else they needed would have to improvise from things found on the planet or would be provided in the crates they would fine at the checkpoints. The students would have only the clothing on their backs and could not bring anything else with them. Each student would go through scanning while boarding the shuttles to verify they were not bringing any unauthorized items onboard.

As the last week went by everyone became more and more nervous about the tournament. Mouse, Ssam and Caalin were constantly going through diagrams of things they could create with items found on the planet. Mouse asked," Do you think we will be able to find what we need to build anything we can use?" Ssam replied, "There are a lot of old mine sites that should have equipment we can salvage." The girls were going through the list of plants and animals that were eatable and frantically trying to remember them. The group had decided that the boys would be in charge of navigation, communication and anything dealing with technical devices. Ang and Ssophia would be in charge of making sure they were able to find eatable food and fresh drinking water.

The day before the tournament everyone received the shuttle assignments. Pods were loaded on each shuttle and equipment was stored onboard. The nerves of the every student were on end. Everyone met that evening in the dining hall to play board games to help get their minds off the next day. Even the Delta squad came to play games and Dargon seemed as nervous as the rest of them. They were all unsure of their navigational abilities and whether they would be able to locate any food sources to keep them going. That night everyone one attempted to sleep but it was a restless sleep. The next morning each of them ate all the food they could at breakfast since they had no idea when their next meal would be. After breakfast, everyone moved to the docking bay to board their assigned shuttles.

Caalin and the rest of alpha group boarded the Ravin Claw their
assigned shuttle and once on board they began to get strapped in. The
landing pod would be dropped from one hundred meters, and then an
auto guidance system will maneuver the pod to its designated location.
Once on the ground they will have fifteen minutes to unload all their
equipment before the pod would lift off and return to space so the shuttle
could recover it.

Everyone was strapped into the pod; the shuttle lifted off the ground,
moved up through the clouds and slowly left the atmosphere. Once all four
shuttles reached open space the dimensional jump engines came online and
within minutes they were in visual range of Keeyontor. A voice came over
the intercom, "thirty minutes to drop zone one." You could have cut the
tension in the pod with a knife and a short time later the voice came back,
"five minutes to drop zone, opening bay doors." Mouse could hear the
whining as the bay doors opened and the roar of the wind outside. Then
the voice for the last time came over the intercom, "dropping in five, four,
three, two, and one." The pod moved toward the rear of the shuttle then
a sudden drop and jerk as the landing thrusters ignited.

The pod slowly cruised down to the surface of the planet and the
landing gear deploy. The pod made a perfect landing and the doors slowly
opened to reveal a chain of mountains a short distance from their landing
zone. Caalin shouted, "We got to go, grab everything and let's move!"
Everyone quickly unbuckled their harnesses and started gathering all the
equipment, quickly moving out the doors and away from the pod. Once
they were clear the doors slowly closed and the rockets ignited once again
lifting off the ground and slowly disappeared into the clouds.

Caalin looked around trying to get his bearings on their location.
They had had been dropped in a small narrow valley. Remembering the
information he had learned about the planet there was only three hours
of day light left. They needed to find a campsite and the first container
with the information needed. The day before the decision was made that
Caalin would be the leader, he said," Ssam you and Mouse scout out a
place to setup camp and get a fire started. The girls and I will do an area
search for the crate with information we need to point us to our first check
point." Ssam and Mouse moved off toward what looked like a cave about
fifty meters from their location. Caalin looked around and found some

rocks to mark their landing location they would be able to find it again since it would be their starting point. Ang took to flight to see if she could spot anything from the air while Caalin and Ssophia did a search from the ground.

After about an hour of searching Ang noticed there were some rocks in a strange arrangement. She flew down to take a look around the rock formation Caalin and Ssophia shortly joined her. Ssophia shouted, "I found a metal box underneath these rocks over here!" Ang and Caalin joined her and they tried to move one of the large rocks off the container. Unfortunately they were unable to do so and with no tools to dig out the box they were at a loss. Ssophia snapped. "I can't believe they put our information under this rock!" Caalin told her that it looks like they set it in a hole beside the rock and something pushed the rock over it. Ang said, "I can fly back to get Ssam and Mouse, but it would take a while to get back." Caalin replied," that would take too long, and they were busy setting up camp." Caalin thought for a moment, "You girls get on each side of me when the boulder moves start pushing as hard as you can." They looked at him funny but did what he asked. Caalin put both of his hands firmly on the boulder closed his eyes and started whispering softly. This went on for about five minutes and the girls were starting to get tired of waiting, then suddenly the boulder began to move. It lifted off the ground about ten centimeters, so girls pushed as hard as they could while all the time Caalin kept his eyes closed and continued to whisper. When the stone was clear of the box Ssophia yelled, "We're clear!" Caalin opened his eyes and the boulder dropped back to the ground. Ang looked at Caalin, "How did you do that?" He said, "We can talk about it later we need to get the box and find Ssam and Mouse."

Caalin took one side of the box Ssophia and Ang took the other and lifted the box out of the hole. The box did not have a lock so it was easily opened. Inside they found five backpacks, a compass, some electronic components, a small laser welder about the size of a pen, a map with their landing spot marked on it and a sheet of paper. Ssophia looked at the paper with numbers and words on," this must be coordinates for our first check point." They took the contents and divided them amongst each other to carry. Caalin carried most of it and asked," Ang will you fly ahead to locate Ssam and Mouse for us?" Ang agreed to while Ssophia and Caalin made their way back to the landing area, once at the landing area they added more rocks to the ones Caalin had already placed to mark the location. They wanted to be able to fine it the next morning. Ang met them at the landing area a few minutes later. She stated," I've located Ssam and Mouse and they have s great campsite set up and waiting."

Ang led them off toward the location that look like a large cave. Since it was getting darker and hard to see Ang would fly ahead every so often to verify they were moving in the right direction. After about fifteen minutes they were at the campsite.

Mouse and Ssam had a nice fire going at the mouth of an old mine shaft that had caved in years ago. There was just enough room in the front of what was once a large opening to give them cover and protection for the night. Entering the site to the smell of food cooking was a surprise. Ssam had found a Caraki laying eggs in a nest. A Caraki is an animal that seemed to be half bird and half lizard and is about the size of an Osteridge. She had laid two eggs which were each about the size of volleyball before she left her nest. Ssam had been blending into the surrounding area so she did not see him as he scooped up the eggs and ran off to meet Mouse. Once back at the campsite Ssam held up the eggs to show Mouse, "look what I have, and the Caraki never knew I was there." Mouse smiled, "well I had some luck too."

Mouse had found some Baca roots; they are long tubular and similar to potatoes found on earth. He had also found some sheet metal. By the time Ang returned with Caalin and Ssophia, Mouse had bent the metal make a pan that they were now using to cook one of the eggs and half of the roots. Ssam stated, "We will save the other egg for breakfast and the rest of the roots for later in case we don't find anything else to eat." Ssam had started a fire by using a piece of goran crystal he had found in the area. He used a knife to strike the crystal at an angle to produce sparks and ignite some small twigs he had piled up. Mouse had pulled some of the coals from the fire and had the roots and egg cooking on the sheet metal over the coals.

Caalin said, "It smells delicious" as they dropped the packs on the ground. Ssam told them, "It will not taste as good as it smells we don't have any spices for it." Mouse chimed in, "I heard you found the items we needed for the next stage." Ssophia confirmed it by saying they had and then asked, "When is the food going to be ready?" Mouse answered, "It is ready now you just need to get a tray." He had several sheets of metal about thirty centimeters in diameter setting on a log next to the coals. Ssam handed each of them one of the trays and spoons he had made from some of the wood he had found laying around. Everyone got plenty to eat and set around the fire talking. Ang asked, "What do we do next?" Ssam stated, "We need to set up a guard schedule. It wouldn't be a good thing if a Caraki wondered into camp. They can be very vicious especially if they find out we're their eggs."

They all set down and decide who would stand guard. The decision was Mouse would do the first three hours and Ssophia would join him during the last hour and a half of his watch. Caalin would relieve Mouse and Ssophia would stand watch with him for an hour and a half then she would wake Ang to relieve her. Ang would be with Caalin for the second half, at the end of Caalin's they would wake Ssam and he would stand watch with Ang for her second half. When Ang's watch was over she would wake Mouse again and he would join Ssam and start breakfast.

The first half of Mouse's watch was boring but after Ssophia Joined him he had time to look around the area better. He managed to find some electronic components in the discarded mining material. After his part of the watch was over he woke Caalin to relieve him. Caalin quickly got up and went to join Ssophia. Ssophia and Caalin were setting next to the fire staring off into the darkness. Then Ssophia unexpectedly ask him, "What do you think about Ang?" Caalin was surprised," what do you mean?" Ssophia explained," Do you think she is nice looking? Do you like her? Would you go to the year-end-ball with her?" Caalin, shocked by the series of questions had to think for a moment, "I do think she is very pretty, I do like her, I guess, and I have not though about the year-end-ball at all." He then asked Ssophia, "Are there any more personal questions you would like to ask? Ssophia laughed at the answers," you are such a boy."

Finally Ssophia got up and went to wake Ang while Caalin stayed next to the fire staring out into the darkness. After a few minutes Ang joined him with a smile on her face. It was obvious that Ssophia had told her about the conversation they had during her watch. Ang set down next to Caalin asking, "Have you seen or heard anything?" Caalin looked at her, "nothing but the crackle of the fire" as he tossed another piece of wood on it. Ang then asked him the question she had ask earlier when they had moved the boulder, "How did you get that boulder to lift off the ground so we could move it?"

Caalin told," I don't why he was able to do it. When I was about three years old my favorite ball rolled under a large cabinet. No one was around to get it for me so I pushed on the cabinet as hard as I could. While pushing on it I was saying to myself move, move and the cabinet slowly began to move. I got the ball and my parents could never figure out how the cabinet got moved four feet from its original position. I've been able to move large objects like that ever since."

Ang told him, "I think you may have some type of psychic kinetic power and if you practice it you should get better at it." He thought for a moment," I don't think it is that, to me it seems like I am controlling the gravity around the object." Ang replied," either way if you practice you may even be able to move larger objects" She looked around and found a good size rock and moved it over between the two of them. She looked over at him pointed to the rock, "concentrate and see if you can lift this off the ground without whispering to yourself and without touching it."

Caalin set there staring at the rock in his mind he was picturing it rising off the ground. Nothing was happening and he finally gave up. Ang pointed at the rock, "do it again and concentrate harder you're not really trying." Caalin tried once more he pictured the rock in his mind lifting off the ground. The rock slowly started shifting in the sand and then slowly started to rise off the ground. Caalin kept thing about the rock lifting from the ground until it was about a foot above the ground. He then concentrated on moving the rock and slowly it moved in the direction he was thinking. He then thought about the rock flying through the air as if thrown and it zoomed over the fire and into the darkness.

Ang got so excited the she leaned over and hugged Caalin yelling, "That was great!" Then realizing what she did she backed up and just smiled as she blushed. Caalin did not say anything about the hug but just gave her a light hearted smile. He told Ang, "I've never done anything like that before and probably would never have thought to try if you had not encouraged me to." The rest of their time together he would move smaller objects around the fire and campsite. He made some small rock orbit around Ang's head and she giggled. They both set around the fire laughing and talking about the things he could do. Before they knew it was pass time to wake up Ssam for his part of the watch. Caalin decide to wake him by making small rocks hover over him and drop one at a time on his head. Ang would laugh every time one drop, as Ssam would brush his head thinking some bug was bothering him. Finally he set up to see what was going on and Caalin let the rest of the small rocks drop in his lap. Ssam jumped to his feet Ang was laughing so hard she was almost in tears. Caalin was trying not to laugh as he let Ssam know he was overdue for his watch.

Ssam got up to move over by the fire and Caalin lay down to get sleep. Soon it was time for Ang to wake Mouse he would need to start breakfast. As soon as he was up she lay down not far from Caalin and dozed off to sleep. Mouse showed Ssam the components he had found around the area during his watch. While Mouse was preparing breakfast Ssam was able to construct four communication devices using the laser welder and the components Mouse had found. They were crude and only allowed two-way communications but they would work for what they needed. After a couple of hours Mouse woke everyone up for breakfast. He handed out the metal tray they had used the night before with scrambled Caraki eggs on them. Everyone downed their eggs as fast as they could because it was slowly getting daylight and they needed to get started as soon as possible.

Ssam put out the fire while Mouse gathered up the trays and cleaned them with some sand. He then packed them in one of the packs from the crate they found the night before. Ssam showed Caalin the communicators he had built while Mouse was packing away the trays. Caalin took one of the communicators then gave one to Ang and told Ssam, "store the other two in your pack we only needed two for now." Caalin would carry the larger pack since the extra weight did not affect him like the others. They all gathered the rest of the gear and made their way back to the landing zone to get their direction right for the next objective.

When they got to the landing location they pulled out the map to look at it. They needed to find the coordinates of their next objective. Ssophia translated the document and located the objective then said, "It looks like we go east" pointing toward a mountain in the distance. Caalin look at her, "you're right but to make sure we get it perfect we need to orientate the map" Ang asked, " what do you mean by orientate the map?" He explained, "There is not just one north on a map there are actually three, true north, magnetic north and grid north. Since we will be using grid north to travel we need to make sure we are going in the right direction. Grid north may be several degrees off from the magnetic north that we get from using the compass." He then showed everyone the scale on the bottom of the map. He took the map and laid it on the ground then took the compass and laid it on the map next to the scale. He lined up the line on the map for magnetic north with the direction the compass was pointing then showed everyone that they actually would be heading toward an opening between two mountains just to the right of the point Ssophia had pointed. Ssophia was surprised, "we would have been way off if they had gone in my direction."

Caalin then looked at the compass to fine what the reading was for the direction they would be traveling. He then took the compass and lined it up with a point on the horizon. He picked an object in the distant and pointed to it," Do you see that tree next to the large boulders, that is where we will stop to check our bearings again. From looking at the map it looks like we have Twenty-five kilometers to travel to our next objective." They all gathered up the equipment and began walking toward the point in the distance.

Every now and then Ang would fly up ahead a little to see what was coming up for them and radio back to Caalin. It was a very hot day and they had already gone through most of their water. Caalin called Ang on the radio, 'will you circle around the area to see if you can spot any water." Ang quickly replied, "I have already started looking." Caalin replied, "Thanks, let us know if you spot any." After about four hours of walking they reached the point they had picked a lone tree next to two large boulders. Caalin pulled the map out and placed it on the ground to orient it again. After he had oriented it he looked at the direction they had to travel, it was through a narrow path between the mountains. In order to stay on the right path and not veer off into any of the small paths that connected to the main one Caalin came up with a plan. He would pick a spot in the distance in this winding path and keep his bearing with the compass. He asked Ang, "Can you take Mouse and fly to a point in the distance then hover over the path? I can then guide you with the radio to line you up. Once lined up you can land with Mouse and we walk the path until we reach you." Ang said, "I can do this on my own without having to take Mouse." Caalin replied," we need to stay as a pair just in case of an emergency; we don't know what we may come across in this passage." Ang smiled, "you're right, it is better to be safe though here." She then grabbed Mouse and flew off in the direction Caalin was pointing. She landed and dropped Mouse off and hovered about while Caalin lined her up with the compass, then the others walked ahead to join Ang and Mouse.

Finally they arrived at a point where the path widened considerably; they had been traveling for over twelve hours now. Ssam commented, "We should be nearing our objective we've been traveling long enough." Just as Ssam had completed that statement they saw a flash of light in the distance. Caalin said, "We need to keep walking in that direction. Ang can you fly ahead to see what it is." Ang took flight as Caalin started running in the direction. Everyone was astonished at the speed Caalin could run even after walking all day. He and Ang both got to the object at the same time and Ang looked over at him and he was not even breathing hard. Ang looking at him, "you can really run." he just smiled, "I've always been able to run like that." Looking around they found another box buried half way in the dirt and began digging it out so by the time the others arrived it was out of the ground and ready to open it.

CHAPTER 21

Friends Helping Friends

When they opened the container they discovered another piece of paper that required translating. Ang translated it, "it has the direction and distance we need to travel." Mouse grabbing something from the box yelled, "Look we have a hatchet and a small shovel now!" Caalin said, "we should go ahead to make camp here before it get dark, Ang and I will look around for food and water while the rest of you look for a spot to setup camp and get a fire started." Ang replied, "I think I saw some plants just south of here and there may be some water there as well." Caalin gathered all the canteens and off the two of them went in that direction. Ang took to flight and Caalin ran along the ground keeping her in sight.

After about ten minutes the came to a green area covered with small bushes and plants. Ang began looking at the different plants for some that were eatable. Caalin was moving along the edge but staying nearby so he could keep an eye on her. He soon heard what sounded like water running over rocks. He called out, "Ang I think I hear water this way." Ang joined him and they moved toward the sound finding a spring coming up out of the rocks. "Fresh clear cool water", Caalin said as he immediately began filling canteens. While they were at the stream Ang spotted some parkan plants, that grow in water and have round roots that are high in protein taste like beef. She started gathering up as many as she could. Caalin finished filling the canteens then took off his jacket and started filling it with the plant roots. After they had as many roots they could get in the jacket they started back toward the campsite.

Since it was beginning to get dark, Ang decided to fly over head to guide Caalin along the way. It took them twenty minutes to get back to the site because of the low visibility. The others had found another notch in the rocks that would shelter them and had made camp. Mouse had already started cooking the baca roots left over from the night before. Caalin opened his jacket, "We have plenty more parkan plant roots you can cook as well." Mouse grabbed a few and Caalin packed away the rest of them just in case they did not find any more food before the next objective.

While they were cooking, Ssophia Jumped, "does anyone else hear that noise?" Ssam replied, "yes and it that seems to be coming our way." Everyone moved around toward the back wall behind the fire. Ssophia took Ang's hand, Ssam grabbed Mouse and they all blended into the wall behind them. Caalin worked his way around the campsite and slipped out into the bushes and down toward the noise. As he eased closer and closer he could hear people talking. Then he heard a voice he recognized it was Clair Tilone. Caalin called out, "Clair is that you out there? It's me Caalin Matthews." After a few seconds she returned with "Yes it is the entire Beta squad." Caalin yelled back, "Keep moving toward the light it's our campfire I will let the others know you are coming in." Caalin move back to the campsite to meet them and told his group it was Beta squad making the noise. They all moved back in around the fire to greet them.

After a few minutes the weary Beta squad came slowly moving into their campsite. Ssophia quickly ask, "Are you all ok?" Clair stated, "We are fine but we've been out of water all day and have not eaten since we landed." Caalin handed Ssam the canteens, "here pass these to our thirsty friends." He then turned to Mouse, "pull out the rest of the parkan roots and put them on to cook." Ang and Ssophia began handing out food to their half-starved friends. Caalin then leaned over to Ang, "We will need to make another trip to the stream tomorrow while the others are breaking camp." They would take all the canteens to fill with water and some of the packs to fill with roots. Ang agreed with him while she continued to hand out food. Mouse cooked up almost all the roots they had and everyone got their fill of food that night.

Everyone decided to exempt Ang and Caalin from watch that night since they were going for food and water early the next morning. Clair and Ssam would pull the first two hours together. Ssam seemed to have a small crush on her so was happy to have watch with her. Ric and Ssophia would have the second watch. Asgaya and Marty would pull the third with Mouse and Sisten covering the last watch and assuming breakfast duty.

Everyone had finished eating their food and was settling down to relax. Clair then told Caalin and the others about their day. It seemed that they started with just a direction and distance to travel which ended about a two hundred meters from the location of the Alpha squad's campsite. They had used up all their water about half way from their landing point and were worried about finding water. They saw the light of the fire when they were looking for a location to set up their camp and hoped it was one of the other groups. She then looked over at Ssam with a smile, "I was very happy that it was your group and not the Delta squad." Ssam seemed to blush when he heard her tell that to Caalin. Caalin asked, "Can I see your new coordinates?" Clair handed him the paper with the information and Caalin pulled out their paper with the direction and distance and his map. He located the Beta group's new objective then he took his information and found the direction and distance to their point and the locations were the same. He then showed all the information to Clair and the others. He looked at Clair, "would your squad like to travel together to the next point to make thing easier on everyone?" Clair quickly said, "Yes, if that is ok with everyone?" Everyone thought it was a great idea and quickly agreed with her.

Caalin excused himself then went and lay down on his blanket to get some sleep; Ang came over and put her blanket down next to his. She whispered, "I told Mouse that we would be over here so it would be easier for him to find us both in the morning." Caalin smiled, "That was a good idea that way he won't make any of the others trying to find us." Ang laid back to get some sleep but before she closed her eyes she whispered to Caalin, "You're doing a great job as our leader and you did the right thing offering to let the Beta squad travel with us." Caalin told her, "thanks but I had thought about it and it was the best for both our groups." Ang closing her eyes, "That is why you're a good leader." She then slowly eased off to sleep as Caalin lay there with a smile on his face then rolled over whispering, "Good night Ang" as he went to sleep.

That evening while on watch Ssam told Clair about their landing and first night on the ground. How he and Mouse had found the food and setup their camp. Clair told him, "we were not as lucky as your team, all we were able to find were a few berries, the meal you shared with us was the first real food we had so far." Then Clair changed the subject on Ssam asking, "Who are you planning to take to the year-end-ball?" Ssam startle by the question said, "I haven't thought about it, I've had other things that keeping me too busy to consider asking anyone." Then Clair just came out and asked, "Ssamuel Ssallazz will you go to the ball with me?" Before he could even think about it he answered, "Yes!" He looked up and she was smiling and staring at him, then she lowered her head, "I have to confess I have liked you ever since the skyracer race, but I had not thought about asking you until Ssophia told me that you liked me too." Ssam was happy he was going to the ball with her and at the same time mad at Ssophia for telling her he liked her. They finished their watch talking and laughing together then Clair went and woke their replacements.

The rest of the night went quietly as everyone pulled their watch with nothing exciting happening. Just before daylight Mouse woke Ang and Caalin. They gathered up the canteens, backpacks and two blankets then made their way off in the direction of the spring. Mouse then walked over and put more wood on the fire as the morning air had gotten a little cooler. After Caalin and Ang had been gone for about a half hour Sisten woke the rest of the groups as Mouse cooked the rest of the parkan roots. Everyone had a quick breakfast, then began breaking camp and packing everything up. After everything was completed they set around the fire waiting on Ang and Caalin to return. Fifteen minute later the two of them came walking back into camp, and not only did they have water and parkan roots but also berries and Tarra fruit. They tossed everyone some fruit and passed out the berries. "This should help get us through the day", Ang said. Sisten gave Ang and Caalin the last of the parkan roots and they quickly ate them so they could get moving as soon as possible.

As Ssam put out the fire Caalin pulled out his map and he and Clair set down, located the points on the map and plotted their course. Caalin stood up with his compass got their bearings and picked a point in the distant. "See that lone tall tree about fifteen kilometers away", he told everyone, "that is our destination." Clair stated, "We should get moving it is getting warmer so we may be in for a hot day."

CHAPTER 22

Graken Attack

They started out over the long flat desert area that lay between the mountains and the forest and everyone could fill the temperature rising as they walked. The sand seemed to shift under every step which made walking a little difficult. Marty looked off into the distant to their left and there was a large cloud that looked like it touched the ground moving their way. He spoke up, "Hey Caalin do you know what that is, it looks like it is moving our way." Everyone look in the direction of the cloud and Sisten shouted, "It's a sand storm we needed to find cover!" They were out in the middle of the desert by now with no place to take cover. Ang took to flight and started looking around the area for some place for them to a shield themselves from the storm. She spotted a rocky area about a hundred meters ahead of them. She landed next to Caalin, "There are some large rocks up ahead we just need to keep moving." He turned to everyone shouting, "Run there is a place to take cover just ahead!"

Everyone started running toward the rocky area Caalin told Ang, "fly ahead and show everyone where to go I will bring your gear." He ran back and grabbed Ang's pack put it over his shoulders and started toward the rocks. Even with all the extra weight and the head start everyone had on him he passed them all as he ran and was the first to reach the rocks. As everyone got there he shouted," put the packs and equipment between the rocks to block the wind then lay up against them and cover yourself with your blanket." Everyone had just got down and covered when the storm hit. The wind blew the sand everywhere even under their blankets. After about fifteen minutes the storm had blown over and Caalin gave the all clear. Everyone dumped the sand off their blankets and began gathering up all the gear. Clair said, "Check your equipment to make sure nothing blew out." Everyone did a quick inventory and luckily lost nothing to the storm. Everyone grabbed their gear shook the dust off, threw it over their shoulders, and packed off it the direction of the tree again. Ssophia looked at Ang, "That was crazy; I have never been in a dust storm." Ang replied, "Me either and I don't care to be in another one."

Finally they reached the tree that was their objective and took a deserving break. Everyone set down, ate some fruit, and discussed the storm they had just survived. While everyone rested Caalin and Clair set down with Caalin's map plotted where they would go from there. The new path would take them directly through the forest. Caalin asked Ang, "Will you fly up and see if you can see how far it is to the other side?" Ang said, "I can", and took to the air. She looked around then returned and told Caalin. "I can't see the other side it is a huge forest."

Clair spoke up, "the objective has to be in the forest itself." Caalin said, "This is going be tricky, we will need to use the compass to keep ourselves on the right path. We will need to send people out head in pairs then line them up with the compass and walk to them and we will have to do this repeatedly until we reach the next objective." Ssam jumped in, "It would be kind of like connecting the dots and will keep us on the correct heading." Clair said, "Looking at the terrain feature on the map it seems the objective is on a small island in the middle of a lake deep in the forest."

Clair turned and told everyone, "the break is over we needed to get moving." They made their way to the edge of the forest. The forest trees were space far enough apart they would be able to maneuver easily and there was very little undergrowth. Mouse laughed, "Making our way through this will not be tough." Caalin would send a couple of people ahead as far as they could go without losing site of them. He then lined them up with the compass in the direction they needed travel and the rest of the group would move forward to catch up. Clair changed out the people every time so as not to tire everyone out.

Finally Caalin and Ssam's turn to be the point people and mark the path. Caalin took the compass and lined it up with the direction they needed to go in then handed it to Clair. The two started walking through the forest as far as they could and still see the rest of the group. After they had made a good forty meters out they heard yelling and the sound of something crashing through the trees. Before they knew it Charlie squad came running out of the trees headed in their direction and right behind them was a large Graken that seem to be extremely angry. A Graken looks like a cross between a bear and a Rhinoceros but larger. It has claws like a bear, two large horns sticking out its forehead and teeth like a saber tooth tiger. They are extremely fierce animals and the most dangerous on the planet. Caalin yelled, "Keep running toward him and Ssam!" He quickly turned to Ssam, "It's time to do your thing and hide them!" As everyone reached the two Ssam quickly told them, "everyone joint hands", and when they did they disappeared into the surroundings. When the Graken came bursting through the trees all it saw was Caalin standing alone so it charged toward him. Caalin could see the drool flying from its mouth as it charged. Caalin looked over at an old fallen tree and all of a sudden it leaped from the ground and hit the Graken in mid air. This caught the Graken off guard and sent it tumbling over on to its back. Slowly getting to its feet it then leaped toward Caalin again and again the tree hit the Graken in mid flight, as it was getting to its feet it was hit a third time by the tree. This had the Graken so confused and shocked that it turn and ran in the opposite direction away from the group.

Ssam and the Charlie group then reappeared from the trees. By this time the rest of the Alpha and Beta squads were running toward them. Ang, Ssophia and Clair, were the first to arrive and were asking, "What had happened?" Jason Rogers told them, "We walked up on the Graken and before we could do anything it turned on us and charged. When we came through the trees Caalin was yelling for us to run directly to him and Ssam." He look over at Ssam, "When we reached Ssam he was able to hide us from the Graken while Caalin fought it off. I couldn't see how Caalin did it from where we were." Everyone looked at Caalin and asked, "How were you able to fight it off?" Caalin just said, "I was just lucky there were a lot of branches around to throw at it." Ang looked at him and smiled, he winked at her to let her know that he had used his newfound abilities to do it.

Clair asked Jason, "What is your team doing in this area? " He told her, "We were making our way through to our objective that should be on an island in a lake near here." Caalin then asked, "Can you point it out on the map?" he then pulled out his the map and Jason pointed to the location. Caalin showed Clair and together they told Jason, "It's the same objective that we have, would your team like to join up with us to locate the lake?" Jason didn't have to think about it twice and quickly accepted the offer. He told them, "It would probably be a lot safer traveling in a larger group." Jason went over and informed the rest of his group they were going to be traveling with Caalin and Clair's groups. Everyone was relieved to hear that since they were not interested in walking up on another Graken. Caalin asked Jason, "Have you all had anything to eat?" Jason replied, "We had some Baca roots last night before but nothing today." Caalin turned to Asgaya and Sisten, "can you ladies give them all some fruit to eat they have to be hungry."

The Charlie group was grateful for the fruit and it did not take them long to eat it. While they were eating the fruit Caalin took his compass and got their direction again and sent Ric and Mouse out ahead to keep them in a straight line. Once they got as far as they could without losing site of everyone they stopped and waited for rest of the groups. When they caught up Caalin could see what looked like a break in the trees ahead. Ang told him, "There is enough room in the trees now I can fly up to look around." Caalin agreed saying" ok but be careful and not to get out of our site." Ang laughed, "You are such worry wart." She then spread her wings and flew up through the thinning trees above them. From her point of view she could see the lake about a hundred meters away. She returned to the ground and reported, "There is a lake straight ahead of us." Caalin pulled or his compass out took one last look at the direction pointed to a gap in the trees up ahead and told everyone to go toward the opening. Jason asked Clair, "Why is Caalin doing the leading are you not questioning any of his decisions?" Clair replied, "Ssam has full confidence in him and I trust Ssam completely, besides they have helped both our teams so I have no objections, he is a good leader."

CHAPTER 23

The Rescue of Delta Squad

After a few minutes of moving through the trees they all came out on a beach along the lake. From there they could see the island about five hundred meters out. Everyone set down on the beach to take a break while Jason, Clair and Caalin tried to figure out how they were going to get to the island. Jason stated, "Even if it was not too far for us to swim we would have a hard time swimming to it with all our gear." Clair said, "We need to build some kind of raft that is the only answer." Ang told them, "I should be able to fly three of the people over one at a time the smallest three Asgaya, Atira and Mouse. I sorry I don't think I could hold up to fly the rest of them, I'm just not that strong." Caalin put his hand on her shoulder, "you are strong and three would be more than enough that would be less to bring over on a raft." Clair said, "Ok we need to build a raft that would hold the rest of us."

The boys begin to look for logs they could use to build a raft while the girls looked for vines they could use to tie the logs together. They found five good logs that were too big for any of them to move by hand. It was up to Caalin with his new abilities to move them. He lifted the first log and everyone stopped and stared as the log seemed to float in the air about a meter above the ground. Caalin told, "You have to stop staring and move it I can't hold it up all day." Everyone snapped out of their state of shock and started pushing and pulling the log toward the beach. Caalin was able to lift each log one by one while the others maneuvered them down to the lake.

Once they had them on the beach he lifted them once again to run the vines around them and strap them together. Caalin new abilities amazed everyone and they kept asking was that how he beat the Graken. Finally Caalin lifted the raft just enough that they were able to slide it into the water to check if it would float and it did. Caalin said, "Ok load the raft one at a time we need to make sure it will hold our weight."

Caalin told Ang, "The first person you need fly across is Mouse then Asgaya and Atira, once those three are on the ground you should stay with them and rest while we paddle the raft across." Ssam and Gahe had made several paddles from branches and tree bark they savaged in the forest. They were passing them out to the boys when Claire looked at Ssam, "I will take one of those please I do know how to paddle." Ssam just smiled as he handed her one then he toss one to Jason who was trying not to laugh.

Ang made her trips back and forth until she had the three smallest people in the group on the island and she stayed with them as Caalin had requested. When she was flying the last one across the others pushed off with the raft and started paddling in that direction. It seemed like it was going to take forever for them to get to the island so Ang after resting for a few minutes flew back out to meet them. Once she reached the raft she told Caalin, "get one of the vines that were not used and tie one end to the raft, I can use it to help by pulling." He did and she began to help by pulling the raft across the lake. Between her pulling and everyone else paddling they got to the island a lot faster. Once they were on the island Caalin looked at Ang, "ok now you need to get some rest, you are looking tired and I don't want you collapsing on us." Ang was about to say she was fine but the look of concern on Caalin's face changed her mind and she went over and took a seat beside a large tree.

Caalin then walked over to Clair and Jason, "we need to look for food and set up camp." The three of them decided Ric, Ssophia, Sisten and Mari would look for food. Jason, Clair, Caalin would look for their next objective and the rest would start making camp and get a fire started.

After searching for a while Jason, Clair and Caalin found the location of their next objective. There were four boxes all of them where marked with each squads logos so each group would know which was theirs. Caalin looked over at the fourth crate, "The Delta group has a box here too so it looks like they will be coming to the island also, and we need keep an eye out for them." They each opened their boxes and retrieved the information from them. They would wait until they were all in camp to translate them. Jason asked, "Do you think we should grab Delta's information and take it with us?" Before Caalin could say anything Clair spoke up, "Do you think Dargon would appreciate us getting his information for him? I don't thinks so. We should just leave it I don't want any problems with that bunch." Caalin stated, "I have to agree with Clair I don't think they would appreciate us touching any of their stuff so let's leave it right where it is."

They made their way back to the beach and to the raft where they met some of the others picking up the last of the gear to move it to the campsite. It was slowly getting dark and as Caalin was picking up one of the packs he look out over the lake and saw something moving in the water. It was the Delta group and they were trying to swim to the island. Caalin shouted, "Jason, get some of the others it looks like we'll have to go out and help the delta group!" He was worried they would not make it across and like it or not they needed to help. Jason ran up to the campsite and got all of the boys.

When they all got to the beach, Caalin already had the Raft in the water. They paddled as hard as they could toward the oncoming swimmers. Ang soon joined them grabbing a vine and pulling as hard as she could in the Delta's direction. The first one they reached was Devolon who was the strongest swimmer of the Delta group. The boys pulled him onto the raft and he collapsed tired from swimming. Next they pull Jon and Dargon onboard while Ang plucked Keyan out of the water and flew her to the raft. They were paddling as hard as they could toward Evalon now but before they could get to her she went under. Jason did not hesitate for a second; he dove into the water before anyone could say anything. He got to Evalon in just seconds and was towing her toward the raft. Once they made it to the raft everyone pulled them both onboard and then turned back toward the island.

The entire Delta group was grateful for the help, all but Dargon. Dargon looked angrily at Jason and Caalin, "We could have made it on our own we didn't need your help!" Evalon gave Dargon angry look, "Dargon you're crazy if that is what you think. If it had not been for Jason I would have drowned." Devolon jumped in, "Evalon is right I was even getting tired and didn't think I was going to make it across myself." Dargon just gave them both and evil stare, "Whatever, we still need to find our objective."

Caalin told Dargon, "You won't have to look I will show you were it is." They finally reached the island and Caalin led Dargon and Jon to the location where they picked up their instructions for the next objective. Jason and the others help the rest of the Delta group to the campsite. The fire was going great at the campsite and as the Delta squad came walking in the girls got all the wet people around the fire to dry out.

Ssam got with Ric, Mouse and Gahe and they cut some small braches from the trees to make spears. Ssam told Jason, "Ric saw some fish in a small pool of water just around a bend on the island. We were going to see if we can spear some of them" As they were leaving Caalin, Dargon and Jon came walking into camp and Ssam shouted to Caalin, "we will be back soon, hopefully with something tasty." Ssophia was making some tea from tichi leaves she had found. Ssophia was telling Evalon, "the tea will help warm you up, plus it is something other than water to drink."

Clair and Asgaya had some of the parkan roots cooking. Keyan said, "The roots smelt great we only had berries to eat since we landed, Dargon was in such a hurry to get to each objective that we didn't have a lot of time to look for food." Clair quickly gave them some of the roots after hearing Keyan's comment. Dargon just looked at her and stated, "I thought you wanted to win." Jon told Dargon, "We do want to win but it was not worth killing ourselves for and you were trying to kill us all." Dargon snapped back, "no one was complaining until now." Keyan replied, "we were you just wasn't listening" Dargon just let out a snarled and said nothing else.

Caalin looked over at Dargon, "Find a spot to bed down everyone will camp here tonight together, you can beat us in the rest of the race starting tomorrow." Dargon went over and set down by the fire to dry out his clothes. Clair handed him some food and he slowly began to eat it. After a few minutes Ssam and the others came through the bushes and into the campsite. They had several fish apiece in their arms. "We hit the jackpot", said Mouse as he walked up with his fish. "We could have caught more but we wouldn't have been able to carry them all." He continued. Jason, Caalin and even Devolon pitched in to help clean the fish. As they got one clean Sisten and Mari would put it over the fire to cook. Everyone had a great meal that night even Dargon but he wouldn't admit it.

After everyone had eaten they all settled down around the fire. Caalin, Jason, Clair and Dargon set down to work out the night watch for that evening. Caalin and Ang would take the first watch then wake their replacements.

Everyone settled in for the night Ang and Caalin set by the fire staring through the clearing over the lake as the two moons of Keeyontor slowly passed overhead. Ang told Caalin, "You're a great leader not everyone would've done what you did helping the Delta group especially Dargon." Caalin replied, "My mom always told me to look for the good in everyone, that most people are not all bad just miss guided. She said that if you show kindness to them that sometimes they might change." Ang smiled, "You have a very smart mother." Caalin smiled, "yes I do." During Jason and Evalon's watch Jason came right out and asked Evalon directly if she would go to the year-end-ball with him. Evalon quickly replied, "Yes I would be happy too." Jason stated, "I've had a crush on you from begin of the school year." The Evalon admitted, "Well I have always thought you were very handsome." They continued to talk about the ball the rest of their watch.

The next morning Ric woke Mouse and Ssam up early and they slipped away from camp to see if they could catch some more fish for breakfast. Soon they returned with several fish and quickly cleaned them and put them over the fire to cook. The smell of fish cooking filled the air as everyone began waking up. While they waited for breakfast they slowly began to pack the gear up. After breakfast Caalin, Jason and Clair got together to compare their information from the boxes but Dargon did not want to join them. Clair looked at the boys, "well it looks like everyone will be going in different directions from this point."

Evalon came over and told Jason their coordinates and they too were going in a separate direction. Jason asked Caalin, "How are we getting back across the lake there are more of us than before." Caalin said, "We will have to make two trips we will break down into two groups with members from each squad on each trip that way no group gets a head start on the others." This idea did not set well with Dargon but he couldn't do anything about it since he was out numbered and even his own group agreed with the rest.

Ang again would fly the smallest across the lake Asgaya, Atira, Mouse and this time she would add Keyan to her trips. The first group on the raft would be Ssam, Ssophia, Clair, Marty, Gahe, Jon and Evalon. They push the raft away from the bank and paddle across the lake. Once they reached the other side Ang towed the raft back across to the second group. Once the raft reached the group waiting they jumped on and began paddling across and Ang flew the last person across. Once everyone was on the other side of the lake they took a short break while the group leaders check their coordinates on the map and got their bearings on the direction they needed to go.

Everyone said their goodbyes and told each other they would see them at the finish line if their paths did not cross again before that time. While everyone was hugging and saying goodbye Mouse gave Sisten one of the radios Ssam had built. He told her, "If you get into any trouble call us"; she smiled and gave him a kiss on the cheek then ran to catch up with her group. The entire Delta group except Dargon told everyone thanks for the rescue and the food. Ang and Ssophia passed out the rest of the fruit they had to everyone and told them they hope they would find some food along the way.

Caalin looked over at Dargon, "Don't push your people as hard as you have been, it is only a race and win or lose the object is for everyone to finish." Dargon just gave him and evil look as his group walked away in the direction they had plotted. Ssam walked over to Caalin, "do you think her will take your advice?" Caalin replied, "I think he will and the rest of his group will make sure he does." Ssam smiled, "yeah I think Keyan will keep him straight."

All the groups had gone in their separate direction and the Alpha squad was on its own again and began working their way through the forest. They finally reached an area where the trees were not as dense making travel a lot easier. As they made their way through the forest Ang and Ssophia kept their eyes open for food and for any danger that may be around them. They picked berries and nuts along the way and finally found a tree with fruit. They gathered what they could of the fruit and packed it away. After about six hours of making their way through the forest reached another mountainous area.

This area was covered with many old mine shafts and tunnels from all the mining operations that was once this planets main income. It now looked like the direction they had to travel would take them through one of the tunnels. When they reached the mouth of the tunnel Caalin told everyone, "let's take a break we don't know how long the tunnel we need to traverse is going to be and I wanted us to get through it as quick and as safely as possible." Ang handed everyone some fruit and they all set down to rest. While they rested all around them they could see reminisce of what use to have been a fairly large mining operation. There was discarded equipment and half fallen down buildings.

CHAPTER 24

The Tunnel

After setting for a few minutes Caalin got to his feet and began looking around through some of the old mining equipment scattered around. Ssam asked, "What are you looking for?" He told Ssam, "I'm trying to find something we can use for light so we won't be stumbling through in the dark." Ssam and Mouse jump to their feet and began looking too, while Ang and Ssophia gathered up the gear. Ssam found two old lanterns but they were empty. After a few minutes of looking Mouse shouted," I found an old can of fuel we can us in the lanterns, but we need to filter it some way to make sure there isn't any dirt or rust in it." Caalin looked around and found some old cloth and an old metal funnel. He used some of his water to wash out the cloth and the funnel then placed the cloth down in the funnel. They ran the fuel through the cloth and funnel into the lanterns. Mouse stated, "Now we need a way to light the lanterns." Ssam spoke up, "we can use a piece of goran crystal and the rag we used to filtered the fuel." Ssam took the rag and a piece of crystal, and then he struck the crystal with a piece of metal he had picked up. The crystal sparked and set the fuel soaked rag on fire, he then took the lanterns leaned it over the burning cloth to light them.

Caalin asked Ang, "Do you think you have the strength to fly Mouse over the mountain?" Ang replied, "I think I can without any problem, but why? He answered, "If the two of you can get to the other side and fined the tunnel entrance on that side you could yell to us and help guide us through. We can travel toward your voice to stay on the right path. No telling how many different tunnels branch off the main one."

Ang thought for a moment, "You're right that's a great idea Mouse and I will make out way over the top while the three of you make your way through the tunnel." Everything was ready now; Caalin packed Ang and Mouse's gear on his back so as not to weigh down Ssam and Ssophia. Ang took Mouse and the two of them flew up the mountain stopping occasionally on large ledges for Ang to rest a little. As the others entered the tunnel Ssophia said, "I wish I was as small as Mouse then Ang could have flown me over instead." Ssam laughed and told Caalin, "She is afraid of tight dark places." Caalin then turned to her gave her his lantern and told her, "Here you go now it won't be as dark for you." Ssophia gave Caalin a haft hearted smile and said thank you. Caalin told them, "I hoped this is a straight through tunnel if not it could get difficult." They entered the tunnel and made their way along the wall. After they were about twenty meters in they came to a fork in the tunnel. Caalin turn and looked at the other two, "Ok the difficulty level has just gone up for us."

Caalin pulled out the compass to get the direction, "Ok looks like the metal tracks on the floor of the tunnel has renders our compass useless for us. The metal is affecting the magnetic arrow of compass so we can't get a correct reading." Ssam stated, "I don't think Ang and Mouse have reached the other side yet either, I don't hear them yelling." Then Ssophia thought of something she had read and thought to herself when we came in to the tunnel there was no wind. She moved to the fork in the tunnel and held her lantern up at the entrance to one of the tunnels and nothing happened. She then held it over to the other tunnel and the flame started flickering. She turned to Caalin, "This is the way to go, and it is where the air is coming through." They turned and made their way down the narrow tunnel to their left.

They soon came to a spot where the floor of the tunnel was made of wood and they could hear running water below. It looked like the miners had built a bridge in the tunnel to cover an underground stream. Caalin said, "We need to take it slow and go across one at the time the wood may be rotten and we don't really know what is below." Ssam went first the wood creaked and popped but finally he was on the other side. He yelled back to Caalin, "I can hear Mouse and Ang at the other end." Caalin yelled, "That's great we are almost through the tunnel to the other side!"

Ssophia was next to cross, again the wood creaked and popped then Ssophia crashed through the wood. Caalin jumped and tried to catch her but it was too late she hit the water below and disappeared with the current. Caalin forgetting he had Ang and Mouse's packs toss Ssam the radio he had and shouted, "Head for the end to meet up with Ang and Mouse and then look for where the spring comes out!" After that he disappeared into the opening hoping to catch up with Ssophia.

He hit the water below and the current rushed him away. The water was not deep but the bottom was extremely smooth so he could not get his footing. He worked his way to one of the walls to slow himself down. As the stream made a turn he could see a light, it was Ssophia and the lantern she had was still working. She was clinging onto a rock that the spring encircled. Caalin yelled, "Hang on Ssophia I'm on my way!" He worked his way over to her and grabbed hold of the rock.

Once Caalin made it to the rock he asked Ssophia if she was ok. She said, "I am but how are we going to get out of here?" Caalin told her, "we will have to let the spring take us out; it had to surface somewhere I hoped." He took the lantern from Ssophia and told her to hang on to him and not let go. Ssophia put her arms around Caalin's neck and gripped so hard she was almost coughing him. They then pushed away from the rock and rush off with the current.

Caalin used his powers to slow them down by concentrating on the walls of the cave as if to move them. This helped them to avoid hitting a rock that was in the middle of the spring. He could move them left and right as they went with the current. Finally they could see light up ahead and then all of a sudden they shot out through the opening dropping about ten meters into a pool. It seemed the minute they hit the water below Ang was there lifting Ssophia as far out of the water as she could and making their way to the bank.

Ang could not lift her completely so it was more of a drag her across the water to the bank. Caalin was having a hard time he still had the extra gear in his pack plus Mouse and Ang's packs and they were filling with water and dragging him under. He could not keep his head above the water and could not concentrate on anything to help him. Then all of a sudden someone grabbed him and with their help he managed to get his head out of the water as they pulled him to the shore.

Once on the bank, he realized Mouse was the one that had helped him. Ssam had made a rope from some vines while they were watching for them to come out of the hole. Ssam tied one end of the rope to Mouse and the other end to a tree. When he saw where Caalin was, he threw Mouse as hard as he could in that direction and, lucky for Caalin, it was the right spot. Mouse had landed almost on top of him, and Ssam then pulled the two of them to the bank. Caalin exhausted from the ordeal look over at his two friends, "Thanks guys I would have drowned without your help." Ssam chimed in, "we could let that happen Ang would have skinned us both alive."

Ang asked Ssophia was she ok and Sophia told her she was fine thanks to Caalin. Ang was so happy to hear that she jumped up, ran over and hugged Caalin as hard as she could. She then said, "You scared me half to death." Caalin replied, "I'm sorry I had you scared but could you not squeeze me to death Ssophia has already attempted that." She let go and sat back with tears in her eye. Caalin looked up at her, "Honestly I'm ok so please stop crying." Ang wiped her tears away then told Mouse and Ssam, "build a fire so they can get dried out."

Ssam and Mouse gather all the gear that Caalin and Ssophia had and went back up to the clearing above the pond. They built a large fire from old wood they found laying around the tunnel entrance. Caalin walked up to the fire, "It will be getting dark in a few hours so let go ahead and make camp right here." Ang told Ssophia and Caalin, "You need to get out of those wet clothes, wrap your blankets around you and set by the fire while we get your clothes dried out." The two of them remove their wet clothes and wrapped up in their blankets to stay warm. Ang hung their clothes by the fire on a make shift rack Mouse and Ssam setup using some limbs. Ssam and Mouse then went back down to the pool to look for food. They found some more baca roots and Ssam cut another spear and was able to spear some fish in the pool. After a couple of hours they made their way back up to the fire and began cooking the food.

After their clothes dried out Caalin and Ssophia got dressed and enjoyed the food with the others. Caalin cleared his throat, "I will take the first watch since I am to awake to sleep right now." Ang said, "I will take the watch with him so you three should bedded down and get some sleep." Caalin moved away from the fire and took a seat on a large boulder. From there he could see the desert they were going to have to cross the next day it seemed to stretch forever. Ang, with her blanket wrapped around her, soon joined him on the rock and asked, "what's bothering you?" He told her, "I should have been more careful in the tunnel, we should have found something to tie ourselves together then Ssophia wouldn't have fallen through the boards." Ang looked Caalin in the eyes and said, "It was an accident, you are a good leader but even you can't foresee every possible problem that could come up. We are a team so it was a team responsibility not just yours." Then Caalin pointed to the desert, "Look that is what we face tomorrow." Ang told him, "I don't see a problem with you as our leader we can d do it." Then Ang eased over next to Caalin put half her blanket around him and said, "It's getting cold and you don't need to get sick on us."

Ang was soon falling to sleep so Caalin helped her up and walked her back next to the fire. She lay down next to his gear and went to sleep. He put some more wood on the fire and sat there staring up at the stars still thinking about what he could have done better. After a few minutes Ssam woke up and looked over at Caalin and asked, "Why didn't you wake someone up to stand watch?" Caalin answered, "Why should anyone else lose sleep since I am not able to sleep." Ssam got up and moved over by the fire next to him. He then told Caalin, "you need to lie down and get some rest we have a long day ahead of us and we can't have you holding us back because you are tired." Caalin looked at Ssam, "you're right" he then rose moved over to his gear took his blanket and lay down near Ang. As he lay down and pulled his blanket over himself to go to sleep he told Ssam, "You're a good friend." He then laid down his head and went right to sleep.

CHAPTER 25

Catching a Ride

Late in Ssam's watch he heard some rustling in the brush nearby so he woke Mouse and Ssophia. He asked, "Do you hear that noise down near the pool?" They both said they could hear it as well. Ssophia said, "I will stand watch if you two want to work your way down to see what it is." Ssam and Mouse agreed and slowly moved down the hill to see what was making the noise. As they worked their way down to a clearing they saw two Petorins a male and female. Petorins are large desert birds about the size of a horse; they are pretty docile and mate for life.

The female had gotten herself tangled in some old fencing that was in the clearing and the male would not leave her. Ssam told Mouse, "If we can capture the female the male will let us capture him just to stay with her. Then we can use them to ride across the desert." "Ssophia and I have ridden Petorins before on Dardaton while on vacation with our parents," Ssam continued. They look around and found some old rope that was still in good shape. Then Ssam blended into the surrounding and eased up to the female. He slowly put the rope around her neck then tied it to a tree, after that he removed the wire from around her legs. Ssam made his way over to the male slipped a rope onto him and tied it to the same tree. He moved away from the birds then made himself visible again. This startled the birds a little so Ssam softly whispered to them as he worked his way back up beside them. He gently stroked each of them on the head and gave them some raw baca root he had in his pocket. After a few minutes they were use to him and Mouse being around them. Mouse had never seen a Petorin before and was amazed at their size. They had long necks, huge horse like bodies and four legs like birds and were multiple shades of brown.

They lead both of the birds back to the campsite then tied them to a tree at the edge of camp. Ssam told Ssophia, "you can go back to sleep and I'll stand watch for a while longer." Mouse also lay down and went back to sleep. Ssam picked up some raw baca root and went back to feeding and talking to the Petorins. After a few hours he woke Mouse again to stand watch. Ssophia woke up as Mouse was getting to his feet so she joined him and Ssam then lay down to get some sleep.

After a couple of hours Ssophia woke everyone up. Mouse cooked some baca roots and everyone set around what was left of the fire to eat. After everyone was finished they gathered up all the gear and packed it away. Then Ssam said, "I have a surprise for you." He then pointed over to the Petorins and told them, "Now we can ride across the dessert." Caalin replied, "There's five of us plus the packs how are all of us going to ride." Ssam replied, "two people plus all the gear can ride at a time on each Petorin, but since you can run so fast for long periods without it bothering you and Ang can fly, I thought the two of you could swap out riding."

Caalin gave him an angry look, "You think Ang and I can split our time riding?" Ssam was stunned, "well it was just an idea." Caalin laughed, "It's a great idea we will be able to travel a lot faster this way." Ssam was relieved, "great let's start packing the gear on the Petorins." Ssam quickly grabbed some rope and made some bridals to use on the animals.

Since Ssam and Ssophia had ridden Petorins before they would set in front to guide the animals. Mouse would ride with Ssam and Caalin would ride with Ssophia. Ang would fly until she got tired and would watch ahead for them. Before Caalin got on he took out his map and got the direction they need to travel it was due east directly into the rising sun. He helped Sophia on to their animal then went over and helped Ssam and Mouse. After everyone was on he hopped up behind Ssophia and Ang took to the sky. They were off out through the low-lying brush and on to the desert sands. The Petorins were fast runners and carried all the weight with no problems.

They had traveled for about three hours without a stop Caalin could see that Ang was getting tired but she wasn't going to admit it. He told Ssophia and Ssam, "Let's stop and give the animals a rest this is a chance for Ang to ride." Once stopped Caalin jumped down and helped Ssophia down. Ssam and Mouse jumped off their animal and Mouse dug out some raw baca roots to feed both of them. Everyone took a break and had some water and the last of the fruit they had. Caalin told Ang, "you need to ride now; I will run ahead and keep us on course." Ang replied, "I am fine I can keep flying it's not a problem." Caalin said, "Since the four of you decided I would be the leader then I am the one to make the decisions so you are riding."

After a fifteen-minute rest Caalin took out the map and compass to make sure they were going in the right direction then helped Ssophia and Ang on to their Petorin. Mouse boosted Ssam on, and then Ssam pull Mouse up behind him. Everyone was ready so Caalin took off with the Petorins right behind him. Ssam leaned over and told Ang and Ssophia, "It still amazes me how fast he can run and how high he can jump" as Caalin would leap over some of the sand dunes.

Caalin ran for four hours without stopping and with the Petorins having a hard time staying close behind him. He finally stopped when he came up on a rocky area shaded by some boulders that seem to shoot out of the ground. Next to the boulders was a small pool of water that bubbled up like a fountain in the middle of a desert. He shouted, "This looks like a good spot to stop!"

They dismounted and gave the Petorins some more baca root and water from the pool. Everyone took time to wash the dirt from their faces and refill the canteens with fresh water. Caalin pulled out the map and compass again took their bearings, then he said, "It looks like we have another three to four hours before we'll be out of the desert, so let's take a thirty-minute break to rest the Petorins."

Caalin and Ang argued about who would ride this time until Ang finally said, "You can ride if you want to because I'm not and nothing you say will make me." Neither of the two rode so Mouse rode with Ssophia and they put all the gear on the male Petorin behind Ssam. They were off again Ang in the sky Caalin on the ground and the rest in hot pursuit behind them.

Every now and then Ang would fly down bop and yell, "you should be riding!" He would laugh and yell back, "Well I think you should be the one riding!" Ssophia shook her head and told Mouse, "Those two like each other, but neither one will admit it to the other." Mouse laughed and told Ssophia, "That's obvious even to me,"

Three and a half hours later they reached another wooded mountainous area and it was starting to get dark. Ssam and Mouse unloaded the gear from the Petorins and released them with Mouse giving them the last of the baca root they had and telling them thanks for their help. The Petorins did not head back out into the desert but moved off to the south stopping once to look back at the group as if saying goodbye. Ssophia and Ang went searching for food while Caalin built a fire. After the gear was unpacked Mouse and Ssam went to help the girls find food.

CHAPTER 26

Almost there

It was dark when everyone made it back into the campsite. After all their searching they were only able to fine some berries. Ang divided the berries up into five groups and passed them out. Caalin set his aside and told Ang, "I'm not hungry right now, I'll eat them later." When he knew no one was watching he packed the berries away in his pack. Everyone was tired from the travel so Caalin quickly setup the night watch. He would take the first three hours then Ssam and then Mouse. Mouse would wake the girls the last hour of his watch and they would look again for food before they broke camp. Everyone quickly lay down and no one had any problems going to sleep. Caalin set by the fire staring out into the darkness. He could hear the Petorins off in the distances calling back and forth to each other in the night. He could see the stars bright over head and his friends sleeping quietly by the fire. Everything seemed peaceful to him as he thought to himself about what tomorrow would bring. If they did not get the information for their finale objective tomorrow and reach it before dark they would not break the school record. He pulled out the map and looked over it in hopes to find out how much farther they had to go to get to the next point.

After studying the map for an hour he determined that it looked like they were only a few hundred meters from their point. He took out the compass and got his bearings on the direction. After a while longer he woke

Ssam for his watch then told him, "I'm going to take a look around I think we're close to the next checkpoint." Ssam gave him one of the radios, "I will keep the fire burning bright so you will be able to find your way back." Caalin slip out of site and disappeared into the darkness. Ssam radioed him to make sure the radios worked and told him to call if he needed help. Caalin replied, "I will let you know when I'm on my way back in."

After Caalin got far enough away from the fire his eyes adjusted to the darkness and he could now see better in the night's light. He had the compass and could barely make it out in the dim light but was able to keep moving in the direction he needed to. He counted his steps to get some idea on how far he had walked. When he reached the point he thought should be their checkpoint he started looking for a clue. After searching for about an hour he found a box marked Alpha and opened it there was a piece of paper with their final objective and the coordinates. He stuck the paper in his pocket and started making his way back toward camp.

On his way back to camp Caalin climbed to the top of some high rocks to get a good look around. From there he could see the camp below but he could also see three other campfires in the distances scattered along the rocks and trees. Caalin slowly made his way back toward camp. He called Ssam on the radio to let him know he was on his way back in and got there just before Ssam woke Mouse up for his watch. Ssam asked, "Did you fine the checkpoint?" Caalin patted the pocket he had the paper in and told Ssam he did but they would talk about it later he wanted to get some sleep now. Caalin lay down and within minutes was asleep. Mouse made his way over to the fire and set down for his watch as Ssam was laying down for some sleep.

Mouse woke the girls just before daybreak and they went to look for anything they could eat. A little later he woke Ssam and Caalin and they began packing up all the gear. The girls came back into camp carrying some more berries but nothing else. Ssophia divided the berries and Caalin again packed his away with the ones from the night before. He pulled out the paper and the map to show everyone the next objective. Ssophia asked, "Where did you get that information?" He replied, "I went out last night and found the checkpoint." He then located the new coordinates on the map it was the gates to Daratora a small city about fifty kilometers northeast of their present location. He said, "If we can make it before sunset we can beat the old record." Then he told them, "last night while I was on my way back to camp I saw the other groups and they are not far away. They are close enough that any of them have a chance to beat us to Daratora." They would need to get moving as soon as possible if they wanted to have a chance of beating the others. Mouse looked at Ssam, "It looks like the other groups made up for lost time from the last time we saw them." Ssam reply, "I hope Clair's team had an easier time of finding food than they did when we first ran into them."

They put out their fire and everyone grabbed the gear. Caalin made sure he had the heaviest of the packs so as not to slow them down. One last look at the map they had fifty kilometers and most of it was going to be mountainous. Sure enough they had only traveled about thirty minutes and came to some steep cliffs they would need to climb and it looked like it was a good forty meters to the top. Ang would fly to the top and carry Mouse with her. Before they took off Mouse said, "I've been doing so much flying with Ang that I'm beginning to get air sick." Everyone laughed then Caalin said, "Ok we need to get started the top is not going to come to us." Caalin, Ssam and Ssophia began climbing Caalin lead and they used the old rope they had used for Petorins as safety lines tied between them. Ssophia was so nervous she kept telling herself, "Don't look down. Don't look down." Ssam started laughing after hearing her and almost slipped. As soon as Ang had flown Mouse to the top she came back down and stayed close to the others in case they needed help. Ssophia said, "I feel a lot better now they you're watch over us." Ang just smiled, "no problem, I can't let anything happen to my friends." It was a tough climb and took almost an hour to complete but they were finally on the top.

Caalin took the compass and got their direction and they were off again. They moved along the ridge then down into the valley below. Three hours of non-stop going until Ang finally talked Caalin into a rest stop. They rested in the shade of some over hanging rocks and Caalin pulled out the berries he had packed away and divided them among everyone but didn't keep any for himself. Ang asked, "Where did you get these berries?" He told her, "I packed them away a while back and just remembered them." She asked, "Why are you not he eating any of them?" He replied, "I'm still ok from the berries we had this morning." They rested for fifteen minutes then they were on the way again.

Caalin was pushing everyone hard he wanted to break the record set by his father, Dargon's father and the Headmaster. He wanted to prove that his team was just as good if not better they theirs was, and this was a record he wanted to break. They moved rapidly through the valley and round a bend. They came around the bend and met up with Beta and Charlie Squads coming down through another valley that connected with theirs. Beta and Charlie squads had linked up about an hour earlier and decided to travel together. Ang asked Clair, "Have any of you seen the Delta group?" Clair replied, "We saw them climbing the ridge about an hour back so they have to be somewhere above us." Caalin told them, "If we stayed in the Valley we should come out ahead of them and if we all stayed together as a group we should beat them easily."

They were moving as quickly as they could through the valley when suddenly they heard some movement in the rocks above them. Jason looked up and yelled, "Rockslide!" Everyone made a run for it trying to beat the falling rocks. Everyone was almost clear when Caalin looked back and saw Sisten and Atira were about to be hit by a large boulder coming down the mountain. Caalin turned and ran as hard as he could which making him almost a blur to everyone around him. He grabbed the two girls and dove with them under an overhang. The boulder and the rocks that came down around them trapped the three underneath.

Caalin asked, "Are the two of you ok?" Sisten was not one of the rocks had hit her leg and it looked like it was broken. Atira had some minor cuts and bruises from the rocks and Caalin had a large cut on his head that was bleeding profusely. Caalin was busy looking for something to splint Sisten's leg but could not find anything. He told her, "You need to set down and stay calm." He had her sit as far away from the loose rocks as she could and be still. Atira tore some rags from her torn uniform and made a bandage to stop the blood that seem to pour from the gash on Caalin's head. She only had minor cuts that had already stopped bleeding on their own so she went over to comfort Sisten while Caalin figured out what to do.

Caalin looked around and found a place where some light was coming through the rocks. He worked his way up to it but it was too small for him to see anything. Sisten reached in her pack and handed Caalin the radio that Mouse had given her. She told him, "Morti told me to use this if there was an emergency and this looks like one to me." Caalin took the radio for her, "Mouse came through for us." He moved over to the opening pointed the small antenna through it and attempted to contact the others. He called out on the radio, "Mouse, Ssam can anyone he me?"

Mouse came back over the radio and quickly, "I can hear you are you all ok?" Caalin replied, "Sisten is hurt it looks like a broken leg. I have the radio antenna stuck out through the small opening so look around to see if you can see it." Caalin pulled the radio back in and quickly tied a piece of cloth to the antenna then stuck the antenna back through the hole. Soon he heard Jason's voice on the other side of the rock yelling to everyone, "I see the antenna over here!" Caalin told Mouse, "I can hear Jason."

The next voice on the radio he heard was Ang asking again was everyone ok. Caalin told her, "Everything will be fine as soon as we can get out from under these rocks. I don't have anything to splint Sisten's leg and we will need some bandages to tie the split to her leg, can you find what we need and try to get it through to me?" He did not tell her anything about his injuries so as not to worry her anymore. She took Clair and Ssam what he needed and they went to gather everything. She asked Caalin, "Can you move the rocks with your powers?" He replied, "That might not be a wise thing to do I can't see how the rocks out there are laying on top and it may cave the rest in on us if I moved any of the others. You'll need to dig us out from out there. Plus it would be too dangerous for everyone else since I can't see where I would be throwing the rocks they may hit some of you." Ang then told everyone, "Start moving rocks we need to get them out Sisten was hurt badly." Everyone started moving all the rocks one by one. Caalin told Ang, "If they can clear enough that I can get my head out far enough to see what it looks like I might be able to clear enough to get us out."

Ang relayed the information to Jason, Clair and everyone else so they concentrated their work on the area around the hole where the antenna was sticking out. They finally made it large enough to pass some limbs through so Caalin and Atira could splint Sisten's leg. Then after a couple of hours they had the opening large enough that Caalin was able to work his way through to see what was covering them. After he took a good look around, he told Jason, "Get everyone clear of the area." Once the area was clear Jason yelled down to Caalin, "all clear!" All of a sudden rocks started shaking and then flew everywhere as if blasted with explosives. There was an opening in the rocks now large enough for everyone to get out. First they got Sisten out then Atira and Caalin.

Once Sisten was out Ang, Ssophia and Clair looked at her leg then adjusted the splint. Mouse and Ssam made it their job to make a stretcher to carry Sisten on since she would not be able to walk. The girls then looked at Atira's cuts cleaning them to make sure they did not get infected. As Caalin made his way through the rocks Ang saw the bandage on his head and ran over to check on him. She was angry;" You didn't tell me you were hurt." She removed his bandage to get a closer look at the injury. Ang could see he was still bleeding badly she told, "you need to set down we need to put a tighter bandage on that before you lose too much blood." Everyone looked through their packs to find enough bandages to use and passed them to Ang. Ang rewrapped his head making it as tight as possible to help stop the bleeding. She asked, "What is your plan now that we have injured people?"

Caalin called Clair and Jason over to talk. He told them, "There is no way any of us are going to break the record with injured people." He Look at both of them and asked "Do you want to finish this challenge as one team?" He continued, "I know you needed to discuss it with your groups but it would be an honor for Alpha squad to finish it with our friends." Clair and Jason looked at each other then told Caalin, "There is no need in talking to the others we know they would be happy to finish with Alpha squad" They then turned and address the rest of the groups and told them what they had decided. Everyone cheered as they were given the news with Mouse cheering the loudest.

Mouse made it his priority to make sure Sisten was comfortable. They placed her on the stretcher and took turns carrying it as they slowly made their way through the rest of the valley and back out on to the flat plains.

It was getting dark when Caalin asked Clair and Jason, "do you want to make camp or push on to see if we can finish in descent time after the Delta group." Jason spoke up, "We should push on we needed to get the injured people help as soon as possible included you. You are still losing a lot of blood." Clair said, "I agree with Jason on this one, we do need to get the injured help as soon as possible." They turned to inform everyone and noticed everyone was looking at something in front of them that was moving in their direction. Caalin looked up and was shocked to see it was the Delta group walking back in their direction.

As the Delta squad came in to meet them Dargon walked up to Caalin, Clair and Jason, "I sorry if our moving through the rocks above you caused the rockslide." He continued, "If you would accept it the Delta squad would like to help and would like to finish the tournament with the rest of you as one group."He then made the comment, "Besides a win is not a win if you are running against an injured opponent." Although Clair was not happy with it they accepted Dargon's offer, mainly because they were all shocked that he would even offer let alone apologize. Devolon and Jon walked over and ask if they could help carry Sisten's stretcher to give the others a break.

Now the entire combined group pushed on into the night and early morning when finally they saw the gates Daratora. As they got closer to the gates Caalin blacked out from the loss of blood. Devolon and Jason picked him up and carried him the rest of the way. It was almost daylight when the weary groups came walking through the gates together. The sentry rang the bell for the end of the tournament. They had finished two hours behind the record but they all finish and they finished as a team. The tournament administrators came running out to meet them and seeing they had injured people quickly sent for medical help.

Three hours later Caalin still a little weak came strolling out of the medical facility and there Ang was waiting for him. He asked, "Why are you not somewhere getting some sleep?" She replied, "I couldn't rest until I knew you were ok and besides someone had to show you where we are sleeping? He told her, "they used twenty stitches on my cut but the doctor told me I won't have a scar and I would survive." The Doctor told me since they don't have the medical technology available that the school does I will need to see the doctors there when we get back. They will remove the stitches and regenerate the tissue around the cut and they would also take care of Sisten's leg then. They said Atira's cut were minor and they and the bruises would heal fine on there on and had sent her on her way earlier." He then looked at Ang and smiled, "We can get some sleep now, then a big breakfast when we wake up I am starving. Ang broke into laughter and lead him off to their assigned sleeping quarters.

CHAPTER 27

The Tournament's End

The next morning Caalin met everyone bright and early for breakfast. As he was loading his plate with food he asked Ssam, "How do you think the headmaster was going to handle the fact that everyone finished the tournament together?" Ssam replied, "It's going to be interesting to see how they rule this one." They then set down with the rest of the groups and spent more time eating than talking.

Everyone was almost finished with breakfast when Professors Taran and Kai walked into the dining facility. Professor Kai asked for everyone's attention and Professor Taran then informed them that the school shuttle would be there in two hours to pick everyone up and return them to the school. He also informed them they were free to walk around the city but would need to be back at the dining facility before the shuttle arrived. Professor Kai walked over and asked Caalin," How are you feeling this morning, you gave everyone a scare when you were brought in unconscious." Caalin quickly told her, "I am feeling fine but how is Sisten?" "She is fine", said Professor Kai "she will see you on the shuttle." She then turned and left with Professor Taran and the two walked back toward the medical facility.

As they were getting up to do some looking around the city Caalin made it a point to go over and thank the Delta group for coming back to help. Dargon sneered, "It was not my idea, the group wanted to help so don't expect me to be happy about it." He then turned and walked off. Evalon leaned over and told Caalin, "The group voted him down he wanted to keep going. The help that everyone gave us on the lake is why we wanted to come back." She continued, "I do not know why Dargon hates everyone, but that isn't the way the rest of us feel."

Caalin then joined the others students and they strolled around the city. As they were passing a small shop Caalin saw a charm on a silver chain in the window and excused himself from the group. He told them."I'll catch up with everyone in a few minutes; I want to look at something in this store." Everyone continue strolling down the walkway. He stepped into the shop and asked the clerk to see the charm. It was a solid silver circle about four centimeters in diameter with a blue Bangalor dragon in the center. He asked the clerk, "Do you have any more of these?" The clerk reached behind the counter and pulled out a box that had six more charms in it. Caalin took five of the charms and paid the clerk by scanning his DNA with the pay scanner and Caalin put in his pass code for his banking account. A pay scanner can scan any part of your body for you DNA then links it with the Alliance database for your banking information for payment. The payment was drawn from an account Caalin's allowance goes into. He quickly put one of the charms around his neck and the others in his pocket then ran out to catch up with the others.

He caught up with everyone just a short distance down the walk. Ang quickly noticing the charm he was wearing, "That is a nice charm it looks just like our squadron logo." He turned to the rest of the Alpha squad and asked,' what do you guys think about it?" They all said it looked like their logo so it was nice. He then reached in his pocket pulled out the others and told them, "I'm glad because I have one for each of you." He handed them each one of the chains taking a moment to put the one for Ang around her neck himself, and told them it was to remember the tournament and the great effort they gave to it as a team. He cleared his throat, "I am proud to be part of such a wonderful group." Both Ang and Ssophia gave him a hug while Ssam and Mouse gave him a hard pat on the back. Ssophia told him, "you did a great job as the team leader even though you wouldn't listen at times," then they all laughed.

They walked around a little more before making their way back to the dining facility. When they returned the shuttle was there waiting on everyone. As they walked up Professor Taran had them go ahead and board. He said, "We are only waiting on a few more people to arrive." They climbed aboard the shuttle and took their seats began showing the charm Caalin had bought them to Clair, Asgaya and Sisten, who had her leg propped up in the seat next to her. Mouse made his way over and took the seat next to Sisten. He asked her, "how are you feeling?" She told him, "I'm fine it hurts a little and I'm looking forward to getting back to the school so the doctors there could fix it right."

Professor Taran boarded and made his way to his seat just outside the cockpit and sat down next to Professor Kai who had been checking off the list of students. The shuttle doors closed and it slowly lifted off the ground and made its way into open space. Once it was clear of the planet they went to dimensional jump and the next thing they knew they were entering the Cat's eye nebula.

Professor Kai announced, "The shuttle will be on the ground in about thirty minutes. Once we have landed everyone should make their way to the dining hall for lunch, your gear will be delivered to the dorm rooms. Those of you who have injuries should go to the medical wing first to be evaluated before lunch" She continued, "after lunch you will have the rest of the day off and the awards ceremony would be this evening after dinner."

Everyone was glad to be back at the school where they knew what was around the next corner. As they walked down the hallway toward the dining hall the conversation was about how they were going to award the trophies if they all finished together. Dargon made the comment, "Delta squad should get first place since we went back to help everyone else." Keyan and Evalon just gave him an angry look for his comment and tried to distance themselves from him. The rest of the groups just ignored the comment and kept moving toward the dining hall.

As everyone tried to eat lunch the upperclassmen bombarded all of them with questions about how things went, who came in first and how tough was the course this year. It seemed like they spent more time answering questions than eating. Soon Caalin and Sisten returned from the medical wing and joined everyone else late for lunch. Sisten was using crutches and told Mouse," They injected medical nanos into my system to repair my leg and it would be better in a couple of days." They had told the others to go on to the dorms, store the gear and get some rest. Mouse and Ang put up some resistance but Caalin and Sisten insisted. Everyone else made their way to their dorms to escape all the questions and to get some rest.

When the group got back to the dorm they set around in the common area relaxing in some of the comfortable chairs. Mouse pulled out a board game but no one was interested in playing so he went to his room to take a nap. Ssam soon joined him to take a nap himself. Ssophia told Ang, "I'm going to take a long hot shower I think I still have some of the dirt on me from Keeyontor." Ang sit alone in the main room until Caalin came through the door and she asked," Is everything ok, are you going to be ok?" After Caalin told her," everything is ok and Sisten will be fine back to her old self in a couple of days." Ang sighed, "Good," then left to take a hot shower herself. Caalin joined Mouse and Ssam in their room, "It feels great to be back in our room away from the thousands of questions. " Ssam said," You're right; now try to get some rest before dinner." They all slowly slipped off to sleep.

CHAPTER 28

Date for the Ball

Caalin woke from his nap about two hours before dinner, took a shower, got dressed, and went into the common room. He was looking over some technical manuals on dimensional jump systems when Ang came out of her room. She set down at one of the desk and began reading some emails from home on one of the computers.

They were setting in the common area alone when Caalin looked over at her, "Ang has anyone had asked you to go to the year-end ball?' Ang raised her head, "no one has asked me, why?" He cleared his throat, "I was wondering." He paused for a second, "No what I really mean is I would be honored if you would be my date for the ball. Would you consider going with me?" A huge smiled came over her face, "I would be happy to accompany you." They set there for another moment then she told him, "I think I'm going to take another shower I think I still have some Keeyontor dirt on me." She slowly left the room, but once she was out of his site she ran to tell Ssophia that he had asked her to go to the ball with him. Ssophia snapped, "Finally! I thought I was going to have to tell him to ask you. I'm glad he wised up without me having to beat it into him." The two girls just giggled at the thought of Ssophia twisting Caalin's arm to make him ask Ang to the ball.

Caalin got up from his chair, made his way back to his room and lay down on the bed staring at the ceiling and smiling. After a few minutes Ssam looked over at him, "It was about time you ask Ang to go to the ball with you." This surprised Caalin and he asked Ssam, "How did you know I asked her? Before Ssam could answer Mouse spoke up, : we were about to come join you, but when we got to the door we saw you and Ang talking, So we had to listen in, besides everyone knew you liked her." Ssam said, "We all could see how the two of you acted toward each other and how you both were so concerned about each other's safety."

Ssam continued, "It was about time, I thought I was going to be the only one with a date for the ball." Caalin was surprised, "You have a date too?" Ssam told Caalin, "Clair asked me the night they stumbled into our camp and we stood watch together." Then Mouse jumped in, "I asked Sisten on the shuttle ride back to school and she said yes too." Caalin Murmured, "Well we all have dates for the ball, but can either of you two dance? I can't." Ssam and Mouse looked at each other and then back to Caalin and both said no at the same time. Caalin just laughed, "Guys I think we may have a problem."

That evening the dining hall was setup differently, all of the freshman class tables were set up in front running parallel to the staff tables and were set facing the rest of the students. As they came in an upperclassman directed everyone to their seats. They were seated boy girl, boy girl all the way down the table by squadrons beginning with Alpha and going down the tables to Delta. The staff came out and took their sets at the main table behind them; once they were seated the food was served. It turned out to be the best meal they had since they arrived back at the school, mainly because they could enjoy the meal without answering a thousand questions. After dinner Caalin noticed a table in the corner with a large trophy and large number medals on it. Once all the tables had been cleared of food and dishes they all turned around to face the staff table. The headmaster stood up and asked for everyone attention.

The headmaster started, "This has been a most unusual tournament, not like any every held by the school. For the first time in the history of the school there was a tie, and not just a tie between two teams but between all of the teams." He continued, "Due to extraordinary circumstances the teams involved this year decided to finish the tournament as a single group and I am proud of them for their actions and decision. The staff and I have discussed the outcome and have decided that everyone involved would have their names engraved on the first place trophy. This is the first time in school history that we will not award anything except a first place trophy." There was a loud roar of cheers from the upper classmates.

After the headmaster calmed everyone he continued, "To honor the heroic decision of the students in helping each other and finish as a single group we are awarding each of them first place medals." He then told the students he would like to show them some video taken by satellites used to monitor the tournament. A large screen came down behind the staff table. The headmaster turning to face the screen, "This video will show you the courage and honor in which this fine group of students conducted their selves. It will also show how some students find things out about their selves that they were unaware of."

The video began and showed thing like Caalin finding out he could control gravity around objects and how he used his newfound powers. One funny example was when he was waking Ssam by dropping rocks on his head. This drew a laugh from the others and Ssam just leaned over and gave Caalin a punch on the arm. Other examples showed how the students used compassion, like when the Alpha group took in the Beta squad on the second night and gave them food. In addition how they protected the Charlie squad from the Graken by the use of both Caalin and Ssam's special abilities. Then it showed the three squads helping the Delta group when they were in trouble trying to swim the lake on the third night. They saw how Ssam, Ang and Mouse helped save Caalin and Ssophia the forth night. The next video showed how the groups saved Sisten, Atira and Caalin from the rockslide and how even Delta group came back to help and how they all finish as one group. Though the Deltas could have possible went ahead without helping and cross the finish line ahead of the rest. The final clip was of the finish of the tournament with Jason and Devolon carrying Caalin across the finish line. Caalin leaned over and said thanks to the two of them and they gave him a nod of acceptance.

After the video the Headmaster turned back around, "Now everyone can see why this was an exceptional tournament and all of these students deserved honors for their actions". After saying that he turned to the table with the medals called up the freshman squads and presented them all awards for courage and valor beyond their calling. He then turned to the rest of the students, "I think this group deserved a standing ovation for what they have accomplished as a group and as friends." The entire student body and staff stood up and applauded the freshman class. That concluded the awards ceremony and everyone in the room filed by and shook the hands of each member of the freshman class while making their way out of the room.

Finally there were no one left except the freshman class and they hugged each other and shook each other's hand. Caalin even made it a point to shake Dargon's hand and tell him congratulations. Dargon just nodded his head and turned away to walk out of the room. Ssam walked over to Caalin and started to say something but Caalin stopped him before he could. Caalin told Ssam, "Just let it go Dargon may eventually come around and see we're not enemies." Ssam came back, "Yeah when my Nam learns to fly a Baametian freighter." Both of them just laughed and walked out the door and back toward their dorm with the others.

As they walked down the hall Clair ran up to Ssam hugged him then told him, "I'll see you at breakfast." As she walked away she turned back and said," Have pleasant dreams." Caalin tried not to laugh but could not hold it back so Ssam leaned over and hit him on the shoulder for laughing. Later in their dorm room common area the boys were getting ready to retire for the evening. Ang came over to Caalin hugged him and said the exact same thing that Clair had said to Ssam. Ssam broke into laughter and Caalin chased him into their room then used his powers to lift him off the ground and hold him over his bed. Ssam yelled," I'll stop laughing just put me down!" Caalin dropped him on his bed and Mouse laughed at both of them and took hits by two flying pillows thrown by the other two.

As they lay on their beds Caalin looked over at Ssam and Mouse asked them, "Why do girls have to be so mushy? Why can't they just say good night they will see you in the morning and be done with it?" Mouse replied. "It's because they were girls and girls are that way." Ssam asked, "What are we going to do about not knowing how to dance?" Caalin told them, "I'll talk to the headmaster about it and see if he has any suggestions. I'll go by the Administrative Office in the morning before class and request a meeting." Ssam and Mouse agree, and then Ssam replied, "The Headmaster should be able to help." They finally settled down and went to sleep.

The next morning at breakfast Clair came over to the Alpha table and set with Ssam. After a few minutes Sisten appeared and set down beside Mouse. As soon as they both were at the table the girls began talking about what they were going to wear to the ball. Caalin interrupted, "Why are you worried about what you're going to wear now it was still weeks away." The girls just laughed at his question and Ang told him, "We have to make sure none of us are going to wear the same thing. In addition we will have to get their gowns shipped to us from home and then fitted."

Ang then turn back to the other girls and begin telling them about the pictures of some beautiful gowns her mother sent her. The boys quickly ate their breakfast and excused themselves. Ssophia asked, "Where are you guys going in such a hurry?" Ssam said," We have to go compare notes on what we're going to wear to the ball." The boys all laughed as they walked off while the girls just gave them angry looks. Ssophia looked at Ang, "And though boys think they are funny." Ang just giggle and they both continued the dress discussion.

CHAPTER 29

Help from the Headmaster

All three boys walked down to the Administrative Office and went in to setup an appointment with the Headmaster. Entering the office Ms Teletora and Ms Serinora greeted them with a cheerful good morning. Ms Serinora looking at the boys, "Dee, don't they all look very handsome this morning?" Ms Teletora reply, "Yes they do Sara" as she turned to Caalin and asked, "Mister Matthews what can we do for you this morning?" Caalin told her, "I would like to make an appointment to see the Headmaster." That very moment the Headmaster stepped out of his office, "I can see you young men gentlemen right now if you would like?"

All three stepped into his office and he told them to have a set. As they were setting down, he asked "What gives me the honor of this meeting so early in the morning?" Caalin spoke up, "Well sir you see the year-end ball is coming up and we all sort of have dates for the ball, but we have one small problem." Headmaster Keayan looked at the three of them, "Let me guess, none of you know how to dance do you?" They all looked surprised that he knew what they were going to say. He continued, "And you would like for me to setup some dance lessons for you, am I correct?" Ssam still surprised, "Sir you're a mind reader, how did you know what we were going to ask?"

The Headmaster laughed, "You're not the first students to have this problem. Caalin's father, Dargon's father and I were in the same position when we were freshmen." He continued, "I will do the same thing our headmaster did for us. I will setup some dance classes for the boys and send everyone the information on when and where later today." Caalin started to say something but the Headmaster stopped him, "I will keep it confidential so the girls will not find out you don't know how to dance." Caalin smiled, "You really are a mind reader sir, thank you very much." The headmaster told them, "ok boys you should be getting off to your classes; I will take things from here." The boys got up and quickly left barely saying bye to Dee and Sara as they went through the outer office.

After the boys left the Headmaster turned to Dee and Sara, "Girls we need to setup another dance class this year." The two just smiled at him and together, "We'll take care of it sir." As he turned to go back into his office he stated, "Remember girls this is top secret."

The boys just made it to universal history class as everyone was taking their seats. Ssophia asked, "Where have you been?" Mouse said, "We just went by the administrative office to check on mail." Before she could question them any further Professor Taran started the class. During class he told them what they could expect on the year-end final and began going over different things they had studied over the semester.

Next in engineering class Professor Marru informed them, "during the engineering final you will have to build four different things. You will have to build them from plans and parts I will be providing." He also informed them, "From now until the finals, I will be giving you plans that you will have to be built in class that day." He started them right away by passing out plans for a dimensional rip generator, used to make a small dimensional hole in space to sent radio signals rapidly for one point in space to another.

By the time lunch rolled around the girls had totally forgotten about the boy's disappearing act that morning. The boys enjoyed a nice quite lunch because the girls had all moved to the Charlie table to talk about gowns again. The boys from Charlie group came over and joined Alpha. Jason grumbled, "If I hear one more thing today about gowns I'm going to be sick." The rest of the boys at the same time said, "We agree with that." Mouse quickly asked, "Do any of you know how to dance?" They all lowered their heads and gave him a low spoken no. Ssam jumped in, "Ok, don't worry, the headmaster is setting up dance classes for us and he will send everyone the details later." All the boys thought it was a great idea and then Jason asked what everyone was wondering, "Who will be teaching the class?" Ssam look over and Caalin shrugged he shoulders, "we don't know yet."

In Politics and Diplomacy Professor EaHaci divided the class into the two nations of Karatora and they recreated the treaty signing joining the two to create the one government. This treaty ended a sixteen-year war that nearly destroyed the planet itself. He informed the students that this treaty and a number of others they would cover would be on the final exam.

Geology and Botany classes where the most boring of all the classes the tedious work of identifying rock and plants.

Finally in Universal language they were translating different languages and dialects from different planets.

Now classes where over Ssam looked at Caalin, "All day spent covering one thing after another to prepare for finals and I'm glad this day is over." Caalin replied, "I couldn't agree with you more, now if we can avoid hearing about ball gowns."

That evening at dinner all the girls set together at a single table this forced the boys to join each other again, just to stay out of their way. They did not want to listen to their ball gown discussions any more. Caalin asked Ric and Marty, "Who are you two going to the ball with." Ric said, "I thought about asking Atira but I haven't been able to catch her alone long enough, she was always with Patrish." Marty said, "I want to ask Patrish but she was always with Atira." Caalin then suggested, "Why don't you go together and ask the girls at the same time." He continued, "Ric you can ask Atira if you can talk to her for a moment and while you're talking to her Marty can ask Patrish." The two boys agreed that was a great idea, they would do it right after dinner.

Ric and Marty set with Caalin and the others until they saw Atira and Patrish leaving. They quickly dropped their food trays off at the cleaning station and followed the girls out the door. As they walk down the hall Ric asked, "Atira can I have a word with you." She said yes and they stepped over to the side of the hallway.

While he was talking to her Marty quickly asked Patrish, "has anyone asked you to go to the ball with them?" She told him, "no one has asked me asked me yet." She lowered her eyes, "I have been hoping one particular boy would ask me though." Marty looked a little shocked and asked her, "Who were you hoping would ask you?" She pointed at him, "you; you knucklehead, you are going to ask me aren't you?" He then smiled and said yes he was. She looked him directly in the eyes and said, "Well ask me Mr. Jiison." He jumped and then stuttered out the words, "PP…Patrish would you do me the honor of going to the ball with me." She smiled and hugged him and told him yes and asked him, "Why have you been so afraid to ask me, I don't bite." He laughed and said, "I was not afraid to ask you, I just couldn't get you alone long enough." He told her, "Well good night, I'll talk to you later." As the two girls walked off he joined Ric to see how it went with him. Ric had a smile from ear to ear, as he turned to Marty, "She said yes." The two boys gave each other a high five and ran off down the hall to their dorm.

CHAPTER 30

Dance Lessons

When everyone got to the dorm the mail was sorted and on the large table in the common room. The Headmaster had the information about the dance lessons mixed in with the regular mail so as not to tip the girls off. The boys told the girls they were going to put on their pajamas and get comfortable, grabbing their mail and heading off to their room. They open the letter from the Headmaster and read it.

"TO ALL FRESHMAN BOYS – DANCE INSTRUCTIONS WILL BE GIVEN IN THE SELF-DEFENSE CLASSROOM THE SECOND AND FOURTH NIGHT OF EACH WEEK PROMPTLY AT TWENTY HUNDRED HOURS, IF YOU FEEL YOU NEED LESSONS YOU ARE INVITED TO ATTEND"

Ssam yelp, "Tomorrow night is the first lesson! Do you think the other boys will be there, other than Charlie squad and us?" Caalin replied, "I don't know we can check with them at breakfast, but we'll have to be discrete about it so the girls don't find out." They quickly put on their pajamas and robes, took the regular mail, and went back out to set with the girls in the common room. Caalin had gotten a letter from home telling him how proud his parents were about his actions during the tournament. There was note in it from his mother saying *I'm glad you came to your senses and asked Angiliana to accompany you to the ball. I think Ang is a very nice and beautiful young woman and you both will look great together. Send me pictures dear.* Caalin looked up from his letter cleared his throat and asked Ang, "How did my mother find out that we were going to the ball together? I haven't told her." Ang looked over at him, "I told her when I wrote her two days after we returned from Keeyontor. I had to let her know you were all right and that the doctors had given you a clean bill of health. I just happened to mention you asked me to the ball in the letter." Caalin just smiled then shook his head and went back to reading his mail.

The next morning at breakfast the girls all grouped together at one table again so this gave the boys an opportunity to talk to each other about the dance lessons. They found out that the Beta boys were going to be at the lessons but they didn't find out anything about the Delta boys. As the three groups of boys ate breakfast they were trying to figure out who would be teaching the class and how were they going to be able to keep it a secret from the girls. While they were all talking Ms Platoron came into the dining hall and asked for everyone's attention. She then announced, "Ladies we will be having meetings on the second and fourth night of each week in the Universal Arts classroom. This will be on the design choices of dresses for the year-end ball and all freshman girls are required to attend these meetings." Caalin lean over and told Mouse and Ssam, "The headmaster thinks of everything, this solves our problem with the girls." They all three gave each other high fives as they laughed at the thought of the girls not knowing anything about the lessons.

Classes went as usual that day every class was to prepare them for the final. At lunch the girls now had a new topic, what was the meetings going to cover about the dresses. The boys were still discussing who would be teaching the dance lessons. With all the talk that was going on the boys could not believe the girls had not heard anything about the dance lessons. That evening after dinner everyone returned to the dorm rooms and the boys waited until the girls left for their meeting before trotting off to the self-defense classroom. They didn't want the girls getting suspicious and start asking questions as to where they were going.

All the boys seem to arrive at the classroom at the same time, and all of the first year boys were there, even the Delta boys. As they entered the room Professor Kai was setting at her desk so all the boys took seats on the rolled up practice mats and waited for instructions. After everyone had taken their seats Professor Kai stood up and welcomed all the boys. She stated, "I am proud of all of you for taking the initiative to learn to dance." She continued, "I would like to introduce my assistances." Right then in walked Ms Serinora, Ms Teletora and Professor Phialiia.

Professor Kai started the music she had selected for the lesson. "This is the same music the band will be playing at the ball." She lined the boys up along the wall, and each of the instructors grabbed a boy by the hand and led him to the dance floor.

They were only teaching them one dance that night so when one boy had the dance moves down the instructor took another boy and started all over again. By the end of the class they had taught the boys the one dance. Professor Kai told the boys, "practice in your rooms, just pretend you are practicing a new self-defense move the body movement is almost the same." The boys rushed out of the room and down the halls to beat the girls back to the dorm. When they got back to the dorm they rushed to set out a game board to pretend they had been playing board games while the girls were out.

When the girls returned to the dorm Caalin ask, "How was the meeting?" Ssophia said, "We looked at several different dresses with Ms Platoron and Professor Fisatoria." Ang commented, "There were so many beautiful gowns. We went over gown colors and fit and we're going to cover make up in these meetings also." Ssophia then told them, "We're going to get to try on some gowns and get to do each other's makeup and hair as well." The girls looked at the boys and Ssophia asked, "Did you have nothing better to do than just set around and play games while we were gone?" Mouse answered, "No, nothing at all." Ang looked at Ssophia and they just shook their heads and went to their room still discussing the gowns as the boys sit in their seats laughing.

The next two days of classes went about the same as all the others every class was to prepare them for the finals. Now it was the night of another dance lesson and the boys were looking forward to dancing with Ms Serinora, Ms Teletora, Professor Phialiia and Professor Kai. One reason was they were not bad on the eyes, they all were very attractive. During lessons Ms Serinora and Ms Teletora seem to argue a lot over who would dance with Caalin. It was so obvious that Mouse and Ssam would tease him about it, but Ssophia and Ang were around the boys pretended to talk about things such as hover-shoes and rocket-packs.

The next night of Dance lessons the boys waited until the girls had left for their meeting about gowns and then made their way to the classroom. Professor Kai had notice during the last class how Dee and Sara argued over who would dance with Caalin, so she had made a roster and gave it to each dance instructor. The roster kept both girls from dancing with Caalin since he was not on their lists. Instead the roster had Caalin dancing with either Professor Kai or Professor Phialiia, which didn't bother him at all because he liked both of them as well.

This lesson they learned how to dance the Barithian Waltz it was a little more complicated than the Pantelian Waltz they had learned the first night. Because of the difficulty of the dance some of the boys managed to step on the instructor's feet, they just could not get the rhythm down. Again Professor Kai explained, "Gentlemen you should move as if it is a new self-defense move you are learning." This seemed to help the boys concentrate on the movement itself and they slowly began to improve. After dance class the boys made their way to the dining hall for a small snack. Professor Kai had arranged to have the dining hall set out snack since she knew that the classes might make the boys work up and appetite. The boy set around having some fruit and drinks and discussed the dance class with each other. They made wise cracks about each other's dancing. Jason said, "It was funny how Gahe managed to step on Ms Serinora feet three times and the look on her face every time it happened." Everyone laughed but Gahe replied, "I don't think that is funny, I am sure it hurt a lot, I'm not a small guy like Mouse." Ssam jumped in, "Yeah if Mouse had stepped on her feet that many time she wouldn't have even noticed." All the boys broke out in laughter at the comment even Mouse.

Afterwards everyone made their way back to their rooms and found the girls already there. Ang asked, "Where have you guys been?" Ssam said, "All the boys decided to meet in the dining hall to talk and have snacks." Mouse stated, "We found out they were serving snacks now in the dining hall for late studiers." Ssophia came back with, "That was nice of them to do that, but I want to know why you three were there having snacks. I know you haven't been studying." The boys just gave them a nasty look as the girls made their way to their room laughing.

With all the classes being preparation for the final the days seemed to flow into one another which made them feel like they were going by fast. It was now getting closer to the end of year tests and the year-end ball. The dance lessons were going great Gahe had finally improved enough that he wasn't stepping on anyone's feet. The night of the last lesson Ms Serinora got over heated and had to step out of the room to cool down. Caalin went to the dining hall and brought her back something to drink. They were standing in the hallway talking and laughing when Ang passed at the far end of the hall and saw them. She was on her way to their dorm room to pick up a picture of her gown she had forgotten. Just before Caalin and Ms Serinora went back into the room she gave him a hug and thanked him for getting her the drink then they both entered the self-defense classroom.

Ang shocked was wondering what was going on, why were they in the hallway and why were they going into the Self Defense classroom. She made it to the room, picked up her picture, and went back to her meeting. When she got back to the meeting she told Ssophia what she has seen. Ssophia asked, "Did you see what was going on in the classroom?" Ang told her, "I didn't want to chance them catching me spying on them." Ssophia then commented, "We will have to find out what is going on, so we'll need to question the boys' weakest link." Then they both said at the same time, "Mouse!" Ang Smiled, "We'll be able to get the information out of him without any problems."

That evening they met the boys in the dining hall for a snack before going to the room. The girls cornered Mouse and Ang came right out and asked, "What are you guys really doing while we're in our meeting?" Mouse nervously told them, "We just meet with the other boys talk and joke nothing else." Ang looked Mouse in the eyes, "Mortomous don't lie to me, I saw Caalin and Ms Serinora outside the self-defense classroom, so what is going on?" She told him, "I wanted to know if Caalin and Ms Serinora are seeing each other." "She is too old for him," Mouse answered. Ssophia jumped in, "that's not true both Ms Serinora and Ms Teletora are from the Planet Malatii and are about the same age as we are. People from Malatii are all taught things while they are still in their mother's womb. Buy the time they are born they have the equivalent of and primary school education. This makes them mature faster than everyone else and by the time they are our age some have finished all their education." "Now why were they together?" she asked.

Mouse finally broke down and told them, "you can't tell anyone what I'm about to tell you; especially any of the boys. If they found out I told you I'll be a dead man." The girls promised they wouldn't say a word to the other boys, but if he did not tell them they would do the killing.

Mouse looked around to making sure no one was watching then whispered, "dance lessons." Ang looked at him strangely, "What!" Mouse shushed her and told them one more time, "The boys are taking dance lessons." He then told them, "None of the freshman boys know how to dance so Ms Serinora, Ms Teletora, Professor Phialiia and Professor Kai are giving us dance lessons. It was hot in the classroom earlier and Ms Serinora over heated and almost passed out. Caalin went to get her something to drink that must have been when you saw them.

Ang told Mouse. "Well, she could have thanked him without hugging him." Mouse looked at her as if he was about to laugh, "Angiliana your jealous!" Ang just blushed and snapped back, "I am not; I just think that Ms Serinora should not be hugging the freshman boys since she works for the school." Mouse just shook his head and went back to join the rest of the boys.

Ang and Ssophia kept their word and didn't say anything to any of the boys about what Mouse had told them concerning the dance lessons. However the word spread rapidly through the girls. All the girls thought it was so nice of the boys to want to learn to dance for them. After the information had passed through the girls they begin to act extremely flirty around the boys. The boys could not figure out why the girls were acting so strange. Mouse, trying to throw off any suspicion that he had told the girls anything, said, "It must be because the dance is getting closer." Caalin looked at Mouse, "Is that what Ang has been watching me so closely? It seems she stares at me every time I get up to do anything." Mouse just laughed, "You can't really explain what girls are thinking." The boys concluded that must be the fact the dance was getting near and just began to ignore them.

It was now finals week and the dance lessons had stopped, it was now the time everyone was dreading, test time.

CHAPTER 31

Finals

Finally Test week was upon them and everyone seemed more nervous than ever. The first test was Universal History and was filled with questions about several treaties, the planetary alliances and planet development that cover thousands of years. The test started promptly at 07:00 and everyone had to turn in his or her papers by 10:30. Students were scattered all through the dining hall so as not to be tempted to cheat. All through the test students were pulling on their hair scratching their heads and rubbing their eyes as the test took its toll on them. Mouse was one of the most nervous of all the boys; this was one of the hardest classes they had. Some students flew through the test with ease, Ang and Ssophia were among those people that turned in their test early and were excused to return to their dorms. The time was running out and some of the students had to rush to finish just before the deadline. Caalin, Mouse and Ssam were among the people that were last minute finishers.

After the test everyone went back to the dorms to clean up for lunch. They all discussed the test and compared answers. As the boys discussed the test the girls would jump in and tell them their answers were wrong just to make the boys worry. Ssophia found it very funny, making them think they had failed the test when she knew that most of their answers were correct. Ssam to Caalin one of the answers he had for a question. Ssophia jumped in, "Sorry to tell you brother but that is wrong" even though the answer was correct. Finally Ang told them, "we've just been kidding with you, most of your answers were correct and you should have passing scores on the test." This still did not make the boys feel any better and the test was still a hot topic during lunch.

After lunch it was time for the engineering test and the boys felt a little more confident about this test. The test consisted of bends of parts that were places at the end of each table. The professor gave everyone three different plans and they had to assemble every item on the plans. After that they had to identify different parts of a phase generator and label them on a diagram. Then they finally part of the test was to explain in writing how a dimensional jump drive worked in comparison to a dimensional rip generator used for communications. This was the test Ang and Ssophia were worried about, it wasn't their strongest subject.

The boys went through this test like a rocket and finished in record time, but the girls on the other hand barely finished before the allotted time was up. Afterwards the test was the topic of discussion for the rest of the evening. The boys wanted to know what each other had to build from the plans they got. Caalin told Ang, "It's impressive that you were able to explain the difference between a dimensional jump drive and a dimensional rip generator." She told him, "The dimensional rip generator just ripped a small hole barely a few centimeters in diameter to allow communications to travel faster through space. However for both of them to work properly you had to have the coordinates for where they were to re-enter normal space." Caalin told her, "You must have been hanging around Mouse so long that your brain just absorbed the information." They all laughed at the thought of Ang learning something from Mouse usually it was the other way around.

The next morning everyone was tired of all of the tests and no one wanted to talk anymore. They were weary. They weren't sleeping well. They were just over it.

Today was the Self-defense test each student would spar with an upper classmate. Examiners awarded points for every defensive and offensive move they used correctly. Several professors scored the matches and the tabulated combine scores were the final test grade. Caalin faired extremely well on this test mainly because of his special abilities. Mouse on the other hand did better than he had expected since he was one of the smallest students in his class. Everyone else seemed to do fairly well on this exam, so during lunch the discussion seemed to cover how funny some people looked trying to do certain moves. Mouse laughing, "Did you see the look n the upper classman's face when Caalin sent him flying?" Ssam jumped in, "It wasn't as funny as funny as the worried look on Caalin's next opponent, who couldn't believe what had happened."

That afternoon the Politics and Diplomacy test was the hardest test they had so far, covering political decisions that had brought down governments and polices that created new governments. Laws that the Planetary Alliance created and enforced that strengthened the traded treaties between planets in the Alliance. The creation and enforcement of planetary travel regulations and policies between planets in the Alliance. Time was up when everyone turned in their tests no one had answered all of the questions on the test not even Ang or Ssophia. They had all skipped through the test answering the questions they knew and then went back and attempted to answer the others. This test turned out to be the one test everyone came out of worrying whether anyone passed it or not.

The next morning they had the Universal Botany test. Each student had a container with several seeds, flowers and leaves from different species of plants. They were required to identify them, list the usages for each and list the planet of origin. They could use micro viewers to look at the molecular make up of the plants. Some of the plants looked almost identical but were different at the molecular level. Compared to the Politics and Diplomacy test this test was did not leave any of them worried about whether they pass it or not.

That afternoon was the Universal Geology one of the easiest classes and this made everyone excited. It was almost identical to the Universal Botany test but with rocks so they knew they would be able to pass this test. That evening everyone was excited over the fact that there was only one more test left to worry about.

The next morning after breakfast everyone sat outside of the dining hall going over translation after translation until it was test time for the Universal languages test. Caalin had a worried look on his face so Ang put her hand on his shoulder, "Don't worry I know you will do well on it." Caalin forced a smile, "I hope so, and I think I forgot everything we went over." The students finally filed into the dining hall, as they were entering each person were required to pick up a large stack of papers. Once they were seated they examined the papers to find that each sheet had a different language on it, and they were to identify and translate each page. That was all that they were required to do, so this turned out to be one the easiest test they were given. Ang, Ssophia and Ssam breezed through the test with ease. Caalin and Mouse had some difficulties but managed to get though the test ok. After the test was over they had two and a half days of free time. Everyone just relaxed the rest of the afternoon playing board games to clear their minds of all the testing. That evening after dinner the boys returned to the dorm room to fine letters informing them they would be getting new dress uniforms and the time for their fittings for the new uniforms. The fitting were by squads and Alphas fitting time would be at nine o'clock the next morning in the school tailor's shop. The school tailor had a small shop just pass the administrative office next to the school barbershop and hair salon.

The boy's woke up early and got dressed; they were setting in the common room waiting when the girls came out of their room. Mouse told them, "it's about time you girls got out here I'm starving." Ssophia replied, "You boys are always hungry and in a hurry so whets different this morning?" They all laughed as they made their way out the door and toward the dining hall. After breakfast the boys went to get haircuts before they had their fittings. While they were waiting for the haircuts they looked at different hair styles on the computer system. They each use the camera on the system to put their picture in the computer then joked around on the system putting different hair styles on each other. After their haircut they went next door to the tailor's shop for their fittings.

After their haircut the made their way to the tailors, this is the location where all uniforms are worked on. They do all the patches and uniform modifications, they take in and let out uniforms for weight gain and loss. At the tailors each of them stripped down to their underwear and stepped in to a scanner. The system scanned their bodies and gave the tailor the precise measurements for the uniforms. The trousers of the uniform had a wide waistband, no pockets and fit snugly to the body. The trouser material seemed to flex with the body so as not to be constrictive. The dress jacket was broad at the shoulders and tapered down at the hip and end at the waistline. This gave the boys more of a V-shape upper body. The color was a dark grey and dark red the Alpha squadron colors. It had the squadron patches and logos on the sleeves and their ribbons and medals would go above the left front pocket. The Tailor showed each of them on the computer what they would look like in the uniform and informed them it would be ready for pickup after lunch the next day.

The rest of the day the boys had skiffer races outside of engineering. The girls were meeting again and trying on their ball gowns to have them fitted properly. Even Dargon and his crew joined in on the skiffer races this time they played fair with no cheating, it turned out to be a great day for all the boys.

The next morning there were more skiffer races after breakfast and then after lunch the boys picked up their dress uniforms and took them to their room. Once in the room they all tried them on just to see how they really looked in them. Mouse looking at himself in the mirror, "Now there is a handsome lad if I ever saw one." Ssam looked over at him, "Well you still haven't seen one." Caalin broke into laughter when Mouse hit Ssam with a nearby pillow.

Once they were all dressed they stepped out into the common room where Ang and Ssophia were sitting and discussing their gowns. The girls looked up at the boys with a look of surprise. Ang staring mainly at Caalin, "You boys look handsome in those uniforms. We would be honored to be escorted by either of you to the ball." Caalin came back with, "That's good because you will be by one of us" as he gave Ang a big smile. Ang with a blush on her face told him, "I'm proud to be your date for the ball and will be the envy of all the girls." This time Caalin blushed and told her thanks. The boys then turned and went back to their room, removed and hung up the uniforms. After putting on their daily uniforms then hurried off for more skiffer racing leaving the girls to their conversation

CHAPTER 32

The Year-End Ball

Finally it was the day of the year-end ball and after breakfast the girls all disappeared. They were all getting their hair done, their makeup done and making final adjustments to their gowns. The boys continued to goof off all day skiffer racing and playing other games. None of the girls showed up for lunch they were still doing the makeup and hair thing. When lunch was over the boys went back to the dorm and just crashed on their beds. Later they heard the girls come in and go straight to their room. A few hours later the boys got up showered and began to get dressed.

The boys stepped out into the common room after getting dressed. Ssam and Mouse wanted to wait to see how the girls looked in their gowns. After waiting for fifteen minutes the two decided they had better go to meet their dates and escort them to the ballroom. As they were leaving Gahe Gluskap was about to knock on the door when they opened it. Ssam quickly told him, "Go on in Caalin is there waiting for Ang." He joined Caalin in the common room and they both took a seat and waited. While they were waiting Gahe said, "What did you think about the crash Dargon had this morning on the skiffer?" Caalin Replied, "I don't know which was funnier the look on his face or the one on Jason's when he flew into him." They were both still laughing and still talking about the skiffer races when the door to the girl's room opened. They quickly jumped to their feet in anticipation.

Ssophia came strolling through the door first and Gahe eyes almost popped out of his head. Ssophia looked beautiful in a creamy light yellow gown and on her wrist was a bracelet with the Bangalor Dragon charm that Caalin had bought everyone after the Tournament. She had taken it off the necklace and put it on the bracelet for the night. Then in walked Ang in a beautiful light blue gown that made her wings look like snow white clouds in a morning sky and her blue eyes sparkled like the stars in a clear night's sky. Caalin could not say a word he was in shock from the site of this beautiful young woman. She also had the charm Caalin had given her on her bracelet. Caalin finally came to his senses, "Ladies it would be our honor to escort you lovely young women to the ball." He held out his arm for Ang to take and as she did he open the door to their dorm room and escorted her down the hall toward the ballroom which was located just down the hall near the dining room.

As they walked through the hall, Caalin kept looking over at Ang with a huge smile on his face. Ang asked, "Why are you smiling?" he told her, "It's because I'm going to be with the prettiest girl at the ball." She blushed and told him, "There will be other girls there better looking than me." Caalin quickly came back, "Not in my eyes." Ang squeezed his arm tightly and smiled as they walked into the ballroom.

As they entered the room they were announce by a tall upper classmate with a very strong voice. He announced them to the crowd, "ladies and gentlemen Ms Angiliana Avora and Mr. Caalin Matthews." Everyone applauded as they both entered the room. He then announced Ms Ssophia Ssallazz and Mr. Gahe Gluskap and again everyone applauded. Once in the room they went over to meet with the rest of their friends. Mouse and Sisten made a cute couple since they were two of the smallest ones in the group. Ssam and Clair looked great together Clair was stunning in her gown and Ssam was smiling from ear to ear. The rest of the freshman class looked great as well; there was Ric Harset and Atira Estanatlehi, Jon Cizin and Asgaya Gigagei, Marty Jiison and Patrish Aningan, Jason Rogers and Evalon Peetora, Devolon Ah Puch and Keyan Vale, and even Dargon Drake and Mari Ekahau. There was not a bad looking couple in the entire group. Everyone was smiling and dancing to every song.

All the girls were surprised at how well the boys could dance even though Ang and Ssophia had let it out to all of them about the dance lessons. But the girls kept it their secret and did not let the boys know they knew. Ang was having a wonderful time and Caalin turned out to be one of the best dancers there, thanks to the lessons. The freshman class danced every dance only stopping when the band took its breaks. Even Dargon had to admit he was having a good time.

At the end of the night the boys walked their dates back to their rooms. When Ang and Caalin got to their dorm they went on in and left Ssophia and Gahe in the hall. Once they were in the common room Ang turned to Caalin and told him she had a wonderful time as she lend over and gave him a huge kiss right on the lips then danced off to her room. Ssophia came through the door humming and dancing on the way through. Caalin was still stunned from the kiss when Ssam and Mouse walked in. Ssam look over at him then turned to Mouse and they both said at the same time, "She kissed him." Caalin snapped out of his trance and looked at the two of them asking, "How did you know?" Ssam told him, "Gahe had the same silly expression on his face and he told us Ssophia kissed him." Mouse popped in and told Caalin, "we were both kissed too." The boys went to their room change into their pajamas and went to bed all with huge smiles on their faces.

CHAPTER 33

Graduation Day

The next morning Ang was waiting in the common room for Caalin and they held hands as they walked to breakfast. At breakfast Gahe set with Ssophia, Clair set with Ssam and Sisten joined Morti, which is what she liked to call Mouse. The girls were still talking about how great the ball had been and how wonderful the boys could dance. Ang and Sophia could not hold it in any more and they told the boys how great it was that they had taken it upon themselves to take dance lessons. This shocked the boys to find out that they knew. Caalin asked, "How did you find out?" Ang just said, "You cannot hide things from us girls we have our ways of finding out." Ssam chimed in. "It looks like a little mouse must have told them," as he gave Mouse an angry look. Mouse popped up, "I can explain why I told them." Caalin looked over at him, "Don't worry about it, the point is we did not make fools of ourselves on the dance floor." Ang smiled, "That is very true, and you dance divinely."

After breakfast everyone went back to the dorms to prepare their uniforms for the graduation ceremony. After getting dressed they made their way to the large auditorium located near the headmaster's office. The girls took their seats in the back of the auditorium as the boys took their positions by the doors. The Families of the graduating class were beginning to arrive and the freshman boys were responsible for escorting them to their seats. Once they had everyone seated they made their way to the back and rejoined the girls.

The graduation ceremony went well; the Council leader of the Planetary Alliance was the keynote speaker. Jason Roger's cousin from Beta squadron was the valedictorian and one of the girls from Delta squadron was the salutatorian. After the ceremony ended the graduating class departed with their families and everyone else returned to their dorm rooms. When they arrived back in their rooms they all found the results of their final exams. Everyone had passed to the next year even though all three of the boys had barely passed Politics and Diplomacy.

Now they were waiting to see what they would be doing during the school break while everyone else was away. Everyone got a two-month break between the year-end and the beginning of the new school year. The outgoing freshman class doesn't get a break between the semesters, they have to stay on at school and help prepare for the next years freshman class. The junior and sophomore students leave the day after graduation on their break.

The next morning at breakfast all of the junior and sophomore students were saying good-bye to each other and after breakfast they all rushed off to catch their shuttles home. The new sophomores wondered the halls of a now nearly empty school waiting to hear what they would be doing next. For the next two days everyone speculated on what they all would be doing to prepare for the next semester. The boys ran skiffer races and the girls set around and recapped the events of the ball.

Two days after the last of the upper classmen had left the school, while everyone was having lunch; Professor Grundor came in and made an announcement, "All students will meet Professor Ravin and I tomorrow morning after breakfast in docking bay thirteen." He then told them what they would be doing during the break. He stated, "We will be taking a trip to Kayousto to collect samples for next year's freshmen's Universal Geology and Botany classes. We will be working in the jungle areas and the dessert and mountainous areas." He told them, "This will be a seven-day trip so they needed to pack wisely for it." Caalin turn to everyone and said, "Now finally something for us to do."

After lunch everyone went back to their rooms and began packing for the trip Mouse packed the radios they still had from the survival tournament. He made it a point to give one to Sisten that evening at dinner. She looked at him and asked, "Do you honestly think we will need these, since we will be with the Professors?" He told her, "You never know they may come in handy." She didn't question him any further and took the radio. The next morning everyone went to breakfast leaving their packs in the dorms. After breakfast they rushed back to the rooms grabbed the packs and then down to docking bay thirteen.

They arrived at the docking bay to find the schools largest shuttle the Star Chaser waiting for them, with Professor Grundor as the pilot and Professor Ravin the co-pilot. Everyone stored their gear in one of the gear lockers onboard and made their way to their stations. Each student was assigned a station to monitor during the flight this was to prepare them for the shuttle training they would begin the next school year. Mouse, Ssam, Gahe, Devolon, Marti and Ric went directly to the engineering station. They wanted to see how the dimensional jump drives functioned. Caalin, Jason, Clair and Dargon went to the Pilot monitoring station. Ssophia, Ang, Patrish and Sisten monitored life support systems. The rest Asgaya, Mari, Atira, Jon, Evalon and Keyan went to the co-pilot monitoring station.

After everyone was at his or her station and settled in Professor Grundor came over the intercom. He informed them, "You will not be doing anything you're your stations you are only monitoring what was going on. We will be lifting off and as soon as they have cleared the nebula they would go to dimensional jump. We will pop out of the jump about an hour out from Kayousto."

As the shuttle lifted off the ground Ssam and Mouse were going over every detail of what was happening with the dimensional jump drive. They knew more about the dimensional jump system than the rest of their class and possibly the class ahead of them. Caalin watched every move that Professor Grundor made. He monitored the gages watched how much thrust he used and how he maneuvered the ship out of the shuttle bay.

The shuttle slowly left the bay made its way up through the atmosphere and into the nebula itself. Ion particles flashed like lightening as the ship made its way out of the nebula. Once they were a hundred kilometers out from the nebula Professor Ravin turned on the dimensional jump engine and contacted the school to inform them they were going to dimensional jump. The school acknowledged their transmission, then with a crack and pop the shuttle was gone. After two minutes of traveling through and array of multiple colors there was another crack, pop, and they were in open space again.

They were an hour out from the planet Mouse explained, "Every ship normally comes out of dimensional jump this far out because of safety reasons. Any closer to the planet and you could crash into a moon, orbiting satellites or ships entering or exiting the planet's atmosphere." Kayousto is an uninhabited planet mostly jungle, mountains and desert but it is a botanist and geologist paradise. It has the largest variation of plant life and mineral deposits than any other known planet.

The shuttle cruised in toward the planet, then through the atmosphere and down to the surface. Once they were on the ground the dimensional rip generator came online for about three minutes then shut down. Mouse told everyone, "Professor Ravin just communicated with the school to let them know that we arrived safely."

They had landed in a location just outside of the jungle area. Once on the ground Professor Ravin came back and opened the cargo bay doors. He pointed to two large containers near the back of the cargo bay and then turned to Jason, "You are in charge of unloading that container." Then he turned to Dargon and told him, "Once they are unloaded you are responsible for setting up the one with the red markings." He told Clair, "You will be responsible for setting up the one with the blue markings." "These are our living quarters while we are here so make sure they are setup properly and make sure they are secured," he said. After that he turned to Caalin and pointed to several containers in the middle of the bay, "those are our transportation while here; your job is to unload and set them up. The other containers contain our food supply and will be unloaded as we need them."

Caalin got the Alpha squad together and they helped Jason's group unload his boxes. Then Jason's group got with the Beta squad and helped them setup their building which was made of a light metal material that unfolded and took form almost instantly. The Alpha squad assisted the Delta squad with their building made of the same material. Then the buildings connected in the center with another large room made of the same material. After the buildings were up everyone helped the Alpha squad with the rest of the crates. They unpacked four large shuttle trucks which were rocket sleds with a large open cargo bed. Once all the equipment was unloaded and setup everyone unloaded their personal gear. The last crate unloaded for the shuttle had their beds that once they were in placed were instantly inflated. They also setup the potable kitchen unit that went in the center part of the buildings.

Alpha and Beta would share one side of the building and Charlie and Delta would share the other. Each side was divided into three sections one for the girls, one for the boys and a room near the center for the professors. Each section had its own set of showers and laundry facilities. Each person was responsible for doing their own laundry. Meals were already prepared in container the just had to be heated and everyone would take turns heating the meals.

After everything had been unpacked and setup everyone prepared and enjoyed their lunch that professor Ravin had heated. After lunch everyone boarded two of the sleds each driven by one of the professors. The professors then gave them a tour of the areas they would be working in to collect their samples. They took them over the desert area, the mountainous region, then over the jungle area and back to base camp. Once they returned to the base Professor Ravin assigned the sled drivers. They were Caalin, Clair, Jason and Dargon and then assigned the areas of work. Alpha and Beta would be collecting planets in the jungle with Professor Ravin. Charlie and Delta would be collecting soil and rock samples with Professor Grundor. He then said, "We will begin after breakfast the next morning so you have the rest of the day to look around."

Everyone boarded the sleds and took off to explore the surrounding area. They hovered just about the trees as they surveyed the jungle scenery. There were colorful birds that flew up around them, unusual animal life and a large waterfall that poured into a small pool with three different streams that rush off in separate directions. They then soared over the mountain and dessert areas and looked at the different colors in the rocks and sand. It too had its share of unusual life forms mostly lizards and small rodents. They made it back to home base just before dark and all settled in for dinner. After dinner everyone set around and discussed the things they saw that day and then wondered off to bed.

CHAPTER 34

Kayousto

The next morning their workday began first with breakfast then out to the sleds. At the sleds they met up with the professors then loaded their needed equipment and lunch on the sleds. After everything was loaded they took their seats. Professors Ravin and Grundor had sky-cycles to ride; this would allow them to move between sites where students were working. Everyone was seated and ready so off they went Professor Ravin and his group in one direction and Professor Grundor and his in another.

Professor Grundor took the Charlie squad to one location and showed them the materials and rocks he wanted them to collect. He then took the Delta squad to another location a few kilometers away and did the same with them. After everyone was busy working he went looking for the new area for next day.

Professor Ravin led his group to a thick jungle area and set them down in a small clearing. Because of the thick jungle canapé they would have to work out from this clearing. He told them there were enough different types of plants in this area to keep them busy all day. He had the Alpha squad moving in one direction away from the sleds and Beta in the other. They were to dig up smaller plants, placing them in containers, label them and put them on the sleds. Once the sleds were full they would take them back to home base and store them in compartments on the shuttle.

Everyone worked hard all morning and at noon broke for lunch. Tired and hungry they all set and ate quietly too exhausted to talk. After lunch it was back to work for the rest of the afternoon. Finally the sleds were loaded with samples and they made their way back to base camp. They quickly unloaded the samples then went inside to get showers before dinner. After dinner everyone was so tired that it was strait to bed and they all were asleep in no time.

The next day was the same as the first day just a different location and everyone was slowly getting use to the work. They were making trips back and forth from the different sites to the base camp to unload samples during the middle of the day. By the third day they were able to return to the base camp unload samples have lunch then go back out for more samples.

It was the fourth day now Beta was leaving the remote site taking some samples back to the base camp. The Alpha squad had put their samples on the Beta sleds and was now loading new samples on their sled. Caalin moved the sled further up in the trees to make it easier to load some of the larger plants they had dug up. As they were loading the plants on the sled they heard a roaring sound like a shuttle passing overhead. Then they heard an explosion in the distance back toward the base camp. They rushed to finish loading the plants and jumped onto the sled. Caalin pulled the sled up out of the trees and started back toward camp.

As they were hovering just about the trees Mouse heard the radio he had brought with him making noises. He dug through his pack and pulled it out. It was Sisten and she was using the radio he had given her before they left school. She was saying something about an attack, the professors being hurt and everyone captured but then the radio went dead. Mouse yelled Caalin land the sled!" Caalin lowered it to the ground in a small clearing. Mouse said in a panic, "There must be something bad happening back at camp for Sisten to call me like that, what should we do?" Caalin pull the sled deep up under the thick jungle canapé in case someone came looking for them. Just as he shut down the engine they heard a small roaring sound and two sky-cycles passed overhead with two strange men on them. They were moving toward the location where they had been collecting samples.

Caalin said, "Those men must be looking for us. We need to camouflage the sled just in case they return." They collected some plant material and covered the sled with it. Caalin then told them, "We need to wait until dark to see if we are able to get closer to camp. We need to see what is going on." They all hid in the jungle staying close to the sled and listened as the sky-cycles continuously pass back and forth overhead.

Finally darkness came and the group uncovered the sled. Caalin told them he would keep it as low as he could and they would have to set down far from the camp so not to be seen or heard. Lifting off the ground Caalin flew sled so low that he was constantly brushing the tops of trees with it. He landed the sled at the edge of the jungle about two kilometers out and they moved closer on foot staying in the tree line.

When they got closer to the base camp they could see two guards walking around the camp. Caalin called everyone close and whispered, "we need a plan but first we need to find out what was going on." He thought for a moment and then told Ssam to work his way around and check out the intruder's ship. "Disable their weapons on it that if you can," he continued, "Ang and Mouse will keep a watch while Ssophia and I check out the buildings to see if we can find everyone." Ssam moved away from the others and vanished into the surroundings making his way toward the stranger's ship. Ssophia then took Caalin's hand and they disappeared as they made their way to the buildings.

When they got to the first building the door was open so they made their way inside. Everyone was down at one end of the room. As they moved further in Ssophia could see a tattoo on one of the men's arms. She leaned over and whispered to Caalin, "I think we are dealing with pirates." Caalin could see two unconscious bodies lying on the floor and realized they were Professor Ravin and Grundor.

Caalin saw Dargon across the room, he was arguing with one of the men who looked like their leader. They moved closer and he could hear Dargon saying, "Do you know who I am? I'm the grandson of Remus Dargon." The pirate backhanded Dargon knocking him to the floor and yelled back at him, "Remus Dargon isn't the leader of the Red Dragons anymore brat!" He then told Dargon, "thanks to you trying to find his grandfather we knew exactly where to find everyone and we will be able to ransom everyone for a large reward." Dargon wiped the blood from his mouth, "when my grandfather finds out about this there will not be a safe place for you to hide." The pirate looked at Dargon and said, "Remus Dargon is probably dead kid, there were rumors he was working for the Alliance so some of the Dragons may have done him in."

Caalin whispered to Ssophia, "We need to make our way over to where Jason and Clair are." Once they were near them Caalin whispered, "Don't make any strange movements it's just Caalin and Ssophia, we have a plan." Jason whispered, "What's the plan Caalin?" Caalin answered, "You need to wait for a distraction outside then jump any guard that stays behind to watch you and make your way strait to the shuttle." Clair whispered, "They shot the professors with a stunner so neither of them will be able to fly the shuttle, let alone get to the shuttle." Caalin said, "Don't worry about the flying just get everyone to the shuttle as fast as you can you'll have to carry the professors." As Caalin and Ssophia made their way back toward the door Caalin told them to be ready and don't stop until everyone is in the shuttle. He quickly grabbed some fruit from a table as they were leaving the building and luckily no one inside saw it disappear.

When they got back to where Ang and Mouse were Ssam had already returned. He told Caalin, "I disabled the ships weapons and I think I got their dimensional jump drive disconnected, but I'm not sure, their ship design is different from any I've seen." Caalin pulled out one of the labels they had been using to label the plant samples. He quickly wrote some information down on it and gave it to Mouse and he then told everyone his plan.

Ssophia, Ang and Mouse would make their way strait to the shuttle. Once they were in the shuttle Mouse would use the dimensional rip generator and sent the message he had just gave him to the coordinates he had written down. Ssam would make his way over to the building and help everyone over power any guards left behind because once Mouse fires up the dimensional rip generator the pirates would come out running. He would take it from there, but first he would have to bring their sled up closer to camp. He then handed everyone some fruit he had pocketed while he and Ssophia were in the building. He told everyone, "get some rest I'm going after the sled" and then he disappeared into the darkness.

About an hour later he came back and was using his powers to hover the sled above the ground as he towed it closer to the base camp. He set it down at the edge of the trees and went over to join the others. Once he reached everyone he said, "It is time so everything will go down when Mouse fires up the dimensional rip generator." He then said to Ang and Ssophia, "Once Mouse sends the message fire up the engines and stand by to close the bay doors as soon as everyone is on board the shuttle. Don't wait on me if I don't make to the shuttle in time jump to the coordinates I gave Mouse." Ang started to say something but Caalin told her it wasn't up for debate.

Ssam took off in the direction of the building and disappeared into the darkness. Mouse, Ang and Ssophia disappeared and went in the direction of the shuttle. Caalin stood in the tree line next to the sled waiting for the rip generator to send everything into motion. After about ten minutes of waiting it all began, the generator fired up and the pirates all began running toward the shuttle. The leader came out of the building and ran toward the others. Caalin jumped on the sled fire it up and ran it straight at the pirates who then turn their attention toward him. He gave a loud yell, "BANGALORS!" as he charged toward the pirates.

There was a loud noise coming from the building then the students came running out and were moving in the direction of the shuttle. The larger boys were carrying both of the professors who were still unconscious. The pirates were firing laser pistols at Caalin as he buzzed them with the sled keeping them penned down. The engines on the shuttle slowly began to whine as they started up. Ssam came out and yelled to Caalin that everyone was on board just as the sled received a hit of laser blast from one of the pirates. Caalin leaped from the sled and with two jumps landed on the ramp of the shuttle as he entered he yelled for Ang to close the doors.

Caalin ran to the cockpit and took the pilot's seat and Ssam joined him in the copilot's seat. Caalin told him to get the dimensional jump drive fired up and then gave him coordinates to put into it. Caalin piloted the shuttle up and through the atmosphere then as they entered space the pirate ship lifted off the ground in pursuit. They pulled further away from the planet and Caalin asked Ssam, "is the dimensional jump drive was online." Ssam told him it was ready and he could activate it any time he wanted.

Caalin said, "Don't do it yet I wanted the pirate ship to get closer." Ssam asked, "Why we can escape the drive on the pirate ship is disabled."

Caalin told him, "That's the point I want them close enough to drag them through with our shuttle." Ssam again asked him why and he told Ssam, "I hope to have a big surprise for them when we get to our jump coordinates and I don't want them to miss it."

Before Ssam could question Caalin any further Mouse yelled, "The pirate ship is about to ram us!" Caalin turned to Ssam, "Ok, you can hit now!" Ssam hit the button, the jump drive activated, crack, pop and they were on their way to the other side. The pirate ship was close enough they were caught in the wake of the shuttle and pulled through with them. Then with a crack they were at their destination and the pirates appeared right behind them.

Before the pirates could do anything a voice came across the communications system, "This is the Delpatara Police Force and we have you surrounded. It would be wise to follow the escort ship to the space dock, failure to do so would result in the destruction of your ship." The pirate ship acknowledged the message and followed the escort ship in toward the space dock.

The commander of the remaining patrol ship then contacted the shuttle and Caalin replied. The voice on the other end said, "Mr. Matthews we received your message and medical personnel will meet you at docking bay twenty two if you will just follow me in sir." Caalin replied, "Yes sir and thank you." He followed the ship in to the space dock and right into the docking bay. The moment they were docked medical personnel were there to assist with both of the professors who were just beginning to coming to.

The students followed them off and were guide to a conference room where Caalin's parents were there to meet them. Caalin's mother ran to hug him then turned to hug Ang and Ssophia. Lord Matthews told the students that they have notified the school and their parents and they would be arriving the next morning. Before anyone could leave the spaceport each one had to talk to an investigator from the Alliance Headquarters. First to talk to him would be Caalin then they wanted to talk to Dargon. The rest of the students set around waiting their turn to talk with the investigator.

While they waited for Caalin to finish Ssam asked Dargon, "why did that Pirate hit you?" He told Dargon, "I saw you talking to that same pirate on Parinta." Dargon looked at Ssam, "Were you spying on me while we were on Parinta?" Ssam came back, "No, I just happen to see you, I wasn't spying." Dargon told Ssam, "Well if you must know I've been trying to find out information about my grandfather; no one has seen him in two years and we don't know if he is dead or alive." Ssam apologized, "I sorry for thinking you were involved with the attack on us." Dargon told Ssam, "Well I've not been very trustworthy, but I am grateful that you guys were able to rescue everyone." When they called for Dargon Ssam slapped him on the back as he walked away, "you're not such a bad person after all." Dargon turned and looked at him angrily, "Maybe but that still doesn't make us friends."

That evening everyone spent the night at the Matthew's home Patora-Blade. Ang was impressed at the size of the castle and the fact that everyone had their own room. The next morning Headmaster Keayan arrived with Professor Kai and part of the parents then later that day the rest of the parents arrived. The Alliance council called everyone to the Grand Hall at Alliance Headquarters. During the meeting at the Grand Hall everyone was told that it looked like parts of the Red Dragons have reappeared throughout the galaxies and the Alliance would be stepping up patrols throughout all the regions.

After some further discussions the Council President then told everyone he would like to present some awards if he may. He called Caalin, Ang, Mouse, Ssophia and Ssam up to the podium. He turned to the audience and told them about the heroic actions these five young students had performed to save their friends and professors. He said, "For these actions I would like to award them all Alliance Medals of Valor." He then turn to the group of young heroes and ask them if they had anything they would like to say to the audience.

Caalin called the group together and they whisper amongst themselves. Then he turned to the Council President and told him that they would like to say something. The President turned the podium over to Caalin. Caalin turn to the audience we only have one thing we would like to say, then the entire Alpha squad jumped into the air throwing their right hand up and clasping them together over their heads shouting, "BANGALORS!" The entire crowd jumped to their feet in applause.

After the meeting they all were standing around talking when Caalin's father called him over. He told Caalin that Headmaster Keayan had decided he was going to give the entire class the next four weeks off before they had to be back at school. Moreover he had talked with all the parents and any of the students that wish to stay and visit on Delpatara could do so and were welcome to stay at Patora-Blade.

Caalin rushed off to tell everyone the news and by the end of the day his entire squad had decided to stay on Delpatara during the time off. The rest of the students went home with their parents to spend some time with Family. During the goodbyes Dargon disappeared without saying anything as his parents were saying their goodbyes. None of the Delta squad had seen him leave and Devolon said, "He is a strange one I don't know if he will ever come around and understand that not everyone is against him."

As everyone else hugged and told each other good-bye Mouse shouted to them all, "We'll see you back at school and then we can tell each other about any adventures we have between now and then."

As they all departed the only words heard were, "See you back at school!"

Printed in the United States
by Baker & Taylor Publisher Services